FLIGHT INTO SUNRISE

AIR PIRATES OF CYRENAICA
BOOK FOUR

BLAZE WARD

KNOTTED ROAD PRESS

Flight Into Sunrise
Air Pirates of Cyrenaica, Book 4
Blaze Ward
Copyright © 2024 Blaze Ward
All rights reserved
Published by Knotted Road Press
www.KnottedRoadPress.com

ISBN: 978-1-64470-417-2

Cover art:
Pixabay.com
https://www.nypl.org/

Cover and interior design copyright © 2024 Knotted Road Press

Reviews
It's true. Reviews help. Even a short one, such as, "Loved it!" So please consider reviewing this book (and all of the ones you've read) on your favorite retailer site.

Never miss a release!
If you'd like to be notified of new releases, sign up for my newsletter.

http://www.blazeward.com/newsletter/

Buy More!
Did you know that you can buy directly from the Knotted Road Press website?

https://www.knottedroadpress.com/shop/

ALSO BY BLAZE WARD

The Jessica Keller Chronicles

Auberon

Queen of the Pirates

Last of the Immortals

Goddess of War

Flight of the Blackbird

The Red Admiral

St. Legier

Winterhome

Petron

CS-405

Queen Anne's Revenge

Packmule

Persephone

First Centurion Kosnett

Encounter at Vilahana

Consensus at Aditi

Hegemony at Dalou

Princes at Ewin

Empire at Gloran

Domain at Yaumgan

Additional Alexandria Station Stories

The Story Road

Siren

Two Bottles of Wine With A War God

The Science Officer Series Season One

The Science Officer

The Mind Field

The Gilded Cage

The Pleasure Dome

The Doomsday Vault

The Last Flagship

The Hammerfield Gambit

The Hammerfield Payoff

The Bryce Connection

The Science Officer Series Season Two

Alien Seas

Buried Among the Stars

Captain Navarre

Dragoon's Honor

Exile

Corsac Fox

Flight of the Corsac Fox

Mistaken Identity

Lords of the Endless Plains

Warlord of the Spinward Reaches

Operation Marrakesh

Trial by Leviathan

Diplomat at Arms

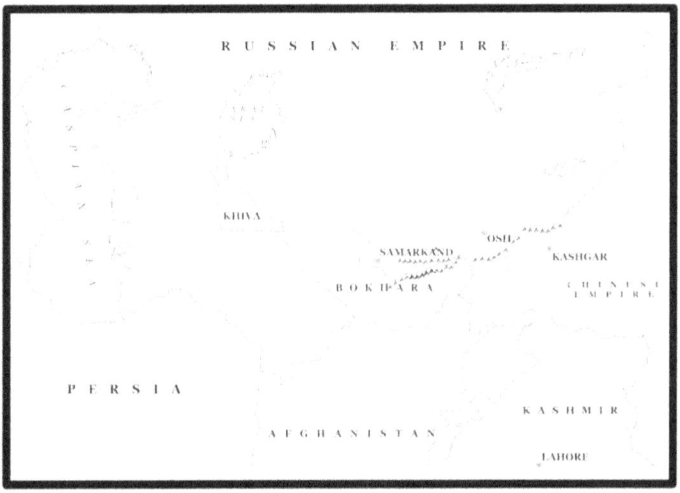

RUSSIAN EMPIRE
KHIVA
SAMARKAND
OSH
KASHGAR
BOKHARA
CHINESE EMPIRE
PERSIA
KASHMIR
AFGHANISTAN
LAHORE

CHAPTER ONE

Late morning.

Sunny.

Pleasant, even.

Finn studied the map as he considered things from the cockpit of his technically stolen California Condor. Once upon a time, a Heinkel H-111 K. Civilian conversion of the Nazi bomber. Great plane, but word had gotten out about the stolen part and he needed a new ride.

Fall was starting and the weather was likely to change soon. Uplands of India wouldn't mind all that much, but he could see the mountains in the eastern distance, that place that really was the top of the world.

Ancient Tibet up there somewhere. Old warrior kingdom ruled by holy men for a long time, though they, the Brits, and the Chinese still bickered constantly about shit.

Not that he could blame 'em. The British were pushing in every direction, trying to extend their Empire to all corners of the map. The Chinese had been weak for a long time, but were finally starting to push back. And maybe then some. Tibetans had been there for a long time and didn't like lowlanders coming in to tell them what to do.

But Tibet was kind of like a walnut stuck in the middle, waiting to see if someone could crack it or not. Toss in the Soviets up top and a variety of folks around Kashgar and those northern deserts that he didn't want to argue with these days, and the whole place was a mess.

Didn't help that outsiders were still all stirred up after what those two crazy explorers, Nicholas and Helena Roerich, had done around here in the '20s. Crazy folks looking for the supposed mysterious city of Shambala. Claimed to have found something, too, but Finn had been assured that to be impossible. At least at the coordinates given by the Roerichs.

And he'd be happy to listen to Asher. Nobody else could read the map they'd found but him. Nor the weird, hieroglyphic symbols on the edges.

Helped, though, that Asher wasn't human.

Fellow was a robot from outer space. *Autonomous Simulated Human Exploration Robot.* Brought to Egypt in 1916, but abandoned after his ship had suffered a failure and crashed.

Everyone aboard had been killed and he'd been left with all his human flesh burned off, leaving only the silver robot underneath.

The Man With No Face, on accounts that he wore an enameled tin mask with gauze inside to keep folks from knowing the truth.

'Cept for his friends.

Finn had studied the old map Asher had found. Rough. Ancient. Hard to understand anything on it, but apparently that was by design. He'd picked up a newer set of old maps from some of Zareen's British Government contacts after she put the fear of God into them boys but good down here in Lahore, where he was currently hiding.

Maps of Tibet were crap, for the most part. Unmapped save by legend. Lots of spots marked *Here there be dragons.*

And they weren't entirely wrong, neither.

Noise outside the plane caused him to look up. Cockpit had

a side window open for whatever breeze might come along. Finn didn't know the seasons well enough yet to calculate the monsoon. Summer one was supposedly over. Winter one was coming. Supposedly, he had a few weeks of calm and dry that he could take advantage of.

Otherwise, they might be stuck here until next summer.

Never a good thing, with the sorts of folks chasing them around heaven and earth.

Finn recognized the car driving close. Big one with the top down, like officials used as staff cars. And he recognized some of the faces inside that he could see.

Airport where they were storing the Condor was out southeast of town. Place the Brits had largely knocked down and flattened, over the complaints of whoever had owned it at the time.

Brits were like that, too. Sometimes well meaning, but a little pushy and full of themselves.

Zareen was half British. Well, half Scottish, which wasn't quite the same thing. Other half was Persian, and nobility on both sides, if not royalty. Finn had never asked too closely.

None of his business. Woman was almost young enough to be his daughter. And that was fine. Him and Hans got to treat her like a favorite niece, while they both watched Emad al-Sadri like hawks.

That fellow would be courting her eventually. Once all this silliness with Asher and the fascists got sorted out.

Assuming Hitler didn't start another war in the next year. Or that fat idiot Mussolini. And the Japs were making their own noises, but that was mostly over in China, where everyone was in at least a three-for-all: Japs, Nationalists, Communists.

Mess. More mess. Might save Tibet for a generation, though, if both sides of China were too busy slapping each other to look this way.

Finn only needed to get in, get out, and get gone somewhere.

Anywhere.

He rose and stretched. Ambled aft through the converted cargo bay and down the steps. Out into the noontime sun that was too damned bright today.

Car rolled to a stop. Folks piled out. Because of the shit he'd been doing all summer and fall, he kept his old Colt 1911 in a shoulder holster under a light jacket, even when he knew all these people.

Else he might have stayed inside and charged one of the California Condor's heavy machine guns.

Ain't nobody going to get pissy when facing that sort of ugliness.

Zareen smiled as she approached, trailed by the others. Hans looked positively happy, which was kinda frightening on the big kraut. Emad was more circumspect, but he'd gone from being a big fish in a small pond to a small fish in a big ocean, and the fellow was still acclimating.

And hopefully he didn't have nearly as many warrants out for his arrest back home in Cyrenaica as Finn did in Chicago and places. Ghada trailed in her appointed role as Zareen's bodyguard, knives all out of sight for now, but a small pistol on her hip like her mistress, though Zareen's was an old Mauser Broomhandle. With detachable shoulder stock in case some rabbit thought he was getting away.

Asher appeared in his usual robes, everything covered up plus a turban and hood obscuring all the metal bits that regular folks didn't need to know about.

Finn found himself kinda surrounded, but that was Zareen coasting to a stop and everyone else circling them like metal dust around a pair of magnets.

He studied Zareen's smile. Seemed promising.

They'd fled Samarkand in Soviet Uzbekistan and hopefully vanished into the aether for a time, aimed northeast like maybe they were headed off to some big-ass crater in Siberia. Tunguska or some name like that.

Nobody ought to come looking for them in the British Raj, though he still slept with his pistol under his pillow.

"Good news," Zareen announced.

The others smiled.

Finn reserved judgment. Something about letting this group out of his sight. Especially the way Hans was grinning. Dangerous something.

Still, he could play a straight man here.

"Oh?" he asked, feeling like the taller half of some old vaudeville act.

"We might have located a replacement for your California Condor," Zareen said brightly.

"Our Condor," he replied automatically. "You're as much a partner here as I am."

He turned to Hans. They'd knocked around together for more than three years now at this point. Fellow knew an impossible number of dirty jokes, but few of them translated out of German worth a damn.

They were the old farts here. Veterans of the Great War in Europe. Both forty these days, with birthdays not all that far away.

Hans was grinning. Still. Bright blue eyes. Blond hair. Tall, lanky fellow. Looked like the Nazi *Übermenschen*. Hated those bastards with the fire of a thousand suns. Even more than Finn.

"And?" he asked the big kraut.

"Oh, I don't want to spoil the surprise, Finn," he chuckled.

Finn sighed and turned back to Zareen.

"Fine," he said.

CHAPTER TWO

Zareen rather enjoyed the way everyone piled back into the car she'd borrowed from some diplomat friends of her father. Hans drove with Ghada up front. She and Emad had sat in back perhaps a bit more primly than entirely necessary, but appropriate, even if Asher hadn't been any sort of chaperone on the first trip.

The addition of Finn didn't alter many equations there. She and Emad had *chatted* on certain subjects, but generally agreed that some decisions would have to be delayed until all this was done.

If nothing else, families would demand to become involved before any sort of romantic endeavors; with her grandmother, the great and terrible Olivia MacQuaid, certainly having all manner of opinions.

Whether Zareen would listen was a different discussion entirely.

But today was about Finn.

Friends had quietly replied to her discreet inquiries with news. She'd snuck Hans off to inspect the options, though everyone knew that Finn would make the final decision. At least Hans could have ruled everything out quickly.

Instead, the jolly German gentleman seemed almost smitten, frightening as that might be.

"Hans, you bastard," Fin groused as they came around a curve and lined up on a particular spot of the airport. "Tell me you didn't."

"I might be lying if I did that, Finn." The man laughed uproariously from the front seat.

Zareen listened to the grumbles, mostly under Finn's breath. A great many profanities generally unfit for mixed company, but she wasn't one to take offense. If anything, Finnley Aart Severijns was proving double his worth as her moral compass. As long as he thought something was still good, she was safe.

It was when she might stray over that line that there would be problems.

And even then, he'd made clear his opinions on outsiders meddling in both Egypt and Persia, so Zareen was confident she could retain him in her employment.

The car rolled sedately to a stop. Finn was out first because she was in the middle. Quickly, the others joined him.

She did not understand aircraft. To Zareen, they were tools.

Hans still retained certain elements of sentimentality for *Cerberus*, the decade-old Ford Trimotor that they had sold to purchase the new California Condor. He might feel the same when they sold the Condor.

Finn just wanted to fly. The Condor, though, was too well known. The German government had put out an All-Points-Bulletin for the plane, as if this was some cops and robbers radio drama, though her British hosts weren't particularly interested in giving those people the time of day.

On any number of topics. What with several new wars in the process of hatching like various demonic eggs.

Hans had given his approval. That had been necessary, but not sufficient.

She fell into Finn's wake as the big American practically stomped over to the new aircraft that was for sale.

Japanese. A bomber of previously unprecedented speed and range, though it still seemed to her that every year brought another revolution in aviation technology. *Cerberus* was hardly a decade old, and already utterly antique by modern standards of speed and power.

She would note, however, that this new model was rather pretty. If you could say that about an aircraft. Twin engines slung under broad wings. Twin vertical tails aft rather than a single one.

Sleek. It gave the impression of incredible speed, even sitting quiescent on the ground resting on the tail wheel.

Mr. Egawa appeared from a nearby hangar where he had no doubt been waiting patiently for her return. Dressed in proper British businessman's attire, regardless of the heat.

Japanese.

Not exactly a diplomat. Not exactly a spy. Not exactly *not* a spy, either.

Her British contacts knew who he was, at least in general, but the two empires, one rising and one already in place, had not yet come into any sort of direct confrontation that caused friction.

Additionally, Zareen had mentioned certain codewords to specific folks, so they had therefore been more than willing to provide her a much more robust briefing on the man, as well as work a bit more assiduously to hide her from the pursuing Germans and that obnoxious Frenchman, Didier Beauchêne.

The world was heating up everywhere, and not just in Germany.

World war was coming.

But not yet.

Zareen stepped past Finn's paused stillness and bowed to Mr. Egawa.

As before, Asher addressed the gentleman in his native

Nihon, which had initially surprised Mr. Egawa—Egawa-san—to no end.

Now, it placed the group in a much more serious, scholarly level.

Asher spoke in Nihon. Egawa-san replied, though both men were fluent in English, as befit a spy. That would be necessary shortly.

She turned to Finn. His eyes were inscrutable.

"Mitsubishi G3M?" he asked Egawa-san without any prelude, but they had prepared the man.

Warned him, perhaps.

"Indeed, sir," Egawa-san replied with a compact grin. "Except that in this case it is a Yokosuka L3Y, a civilian variant originally designed as a VIP transport rather than a bomber. If I may be so bold, rather much like your own Heinkel H-111 K."

Zareen had no doubts that the Japanese would be quite interested in owning their own copy of a German bomber, if only to determine what the state of Nazi technological sophistication was at present.

She suspected that even if they continued to be an Axis of nations, they would eventually fall out with one another. Evil always turns on itself eventually.

"Everything inside is in Japanese?" Finn pressed, still a bit ruffled.

"*Ja*," Hans broke in. "Asher can read it all and we can paint new markings where we need to in English. Mostly numbers anyway."

Finn turned his scowl to her. It had been her assignment, after all, to find them a new aircraft.

He obviously hadn't dreamed big enough.

She smiled up at him.

"No service stations where we're going," he stated ambiguously, not willing to say much in front of a witness and spy. "Got the range and ceiling for this?"

"Over four thousand kilometers range, as I understand it,"

she said, nodding to Egawa-san, who nodded back. "Top speed of three hundred and seventy-five kph. Ceiling above nine thousand meters. Armed, but not as armed as the military model. Inadequacies I should address?"

He stewed. A most amazingly stubborn man, until he came 'round to a certain line of thought, then brutally direct without being offensive, in that way that only the Americans seem to have mastered.

"I think me, Asher, and the gentleman here need to take it up for a flight," Finn said. "Then I'll let you know."

CHAPTER THREE

Asher had not quite understood Finn's apprehension at the cockpit layout, but had gotten everything sorted out quickly. Unlike many aircraft, perhaps a standard if he was understanding the vocabulary here, the pilot of the L3Y sat on the right, with the copilot on the left and the reconnaissance observer directly behind the copilot, where he could no doubt operate radios and such in flight.

Depending on their various intermediate stops, and the technological sophistication therein, Asher might take that spot. He could, after all, speak every language on this planet that was known by more than a few hundred people.

Hopefully, only a few languages of the subcontinental Raj and Tibetan would be necessary for now.

Afterwards...

Asher had no idea what they would find when they arrived at the destination. Or if it would be abandoned.

Or not.

"Everybody stand by," Finn announced as he opened the throttles.

This aircraft was quieter than the Heinkel.

Asher was acting as copilot, though he had never flown any

air or space craft. He was a sociologist, not an engineer or action hero from some radio drama.

Regardless of the current situation.

Egawa-san sat behind him and smiled broadly as the craft began to roll.

The Heinkel could attain and sustain a higher top speed, but had barely half the range and didn't climb as quickly. Nor as high.

Elevation would be important where they were going.

Asher watched. He had explained things to Finn, but the man had quickly grasped all the dials and gauges. At this point, Asher was a tour guide, more than anything.

The plane lifted with a feeling of power missing from *Cerberus* or even Finn's California Condor. The sky was a clear, gorgeous expanse. Everyone fell into something of a lulled silence as Finn committed piloting.

"Questions, Mr. Severijns?" Egawa-san asked.

"Call me Finn," the man replied automatically.

"Finn," Egawa-san noted.

"Handles like a dream," Finn called over the sound of the engines. "How'd you come to be in possession of a Japanese Navy bomber, converted to civilian use, for sale, anyway?"

Asher had wondered as well, but his normal programming precluded him from that level of offensive bluntness. At least without a reason.

He turned back to look at the gentleman in question.

Egawa-san was all smiles.

"Technically, this is a reasonably modified prototype craft," Egawa-san replied. "And, having completed testing, no longer necessary to the authorities. Similar to the Mitsubishi G3M1-L that is going into general service, but currently a VIP transport, as noted. However, the owner expressed an extreme interest in your Heinkel when it was known to be for sale."

"You a spy?" Finn asked.

Asher would have caught his breath, had he lungs with

which to do so. Instead, he allowed a small *blep* of sound to emerge.

"Are you, Finn?" Egawa-san countered, using a verbal Aikido.

"Criminal, maybe," Finn answered. "Gangster, depending on which jurisdiction you ask, back in the States. Only people mad at me right now are the Italians. Maybe a few Germans, but they started it. You didn't answer my question."

"I am a legitimate businessman, Finn," Egawa-san replied sagely. "Who happens to have an aircraft for sale, at a time when you have an aircraft for sale. Both are civilian adaptations of military models, and will serve each other's needs appropriately."

"You flying it back to Tokyo and dismantling it?" Finn laughed. "See what the Nazis are doing. Or were, two years ago?"

"I am not privy to such information, Finn," Egawa-san replied. "However, I would also not be surprised."

"Perhaps you were aware that the Nationalist Chinese Army acquired a handful of roughly identical craft from Berlin?" Asher asked now, intrigued.

"I was," Egawa-san nodded. "And I seem to have heard vague rumors of a presumably stolen German bomber that recently made the Italians look foolish in Libya. More foolish."

Asher nodded but didn't expand. Technically, several flavors of air piracy, but Finn himself had laughingly referred to the collected group as the *Air Pirates of Cyrenaica* more than once.

Asher liked to think that they had simply gotten a head start on the broader war that everyone expected to arrive soon. He had certainly chosen sides, even though such a thing violated so much of his original programming.

At the same time, saving Humanity itself from some greater conflagration fell into the range of not injuring any human through action or inaction.

Inaction was the key. He could stand around and watch the

world go to hell in a handbasket, to use one of Finn's favorite colloquialisms. Or he could reinterpret gaps in his original programming to prevent humanity from coming to injury as a result of his inaction.

The Durren were likely to dismantle his chassis and drain every tidbit of knowledge from his datacore when they eventually realized that he was here on this planet, anyway.

His very existence was a crime, after all.

But he could at least *try* to save humanity.

Asher turned back to Finn. Noted the gruff smile on the man's face as he flew.

Finn would help him save humanity. As would the others. In fact, they were the ones doing the work, and a mere robot like him was simply along as a scholar.

Zareen Vüsala Shirazi would save the world. Or damn it. Many of the current empires—British, Russian, American, Japanese, and others—would not take well to her intent to end imperialism entirely, that the various localities currently under threat of colonialism could achieve their own liberation.

Cyrenaica, for example, en route to all of Persia.

Finn glanced over.

"You're awful quiet," he said.

Asher was normally reticent, so he interpreted that as Finn's way of eliciting an opinion.

"Given the technological status, I find this craft at least as formidable as the Condor, Finn," he replied. "And better in a few places where such things will be necessary."

"Good," Finn said, suddenly standing the aircraft on one wing and starting a powerful descent. "Mr. Egawa, I think we've got a deal, just as soon as Hans can look at the engines."

Asher nodded.

He would have smiled, if he still had lips.

The mad chase across southwest and southern Asia was drawing to a close.

Finally.

CHAPTER FOUR

Didier studied his...companions. He supposed at this point he could call them that.

Bertrand had long since fully healed from his wounds, after having been shot in the back by the American gangster, though supposedly intentionally winged rather than killed outright.

It was the pair of Germans he would have liked to have done without.

"You are certain?" he asked the male.

Herr Doctor Konrad Schwarzenberg. Scientist. Intellectual. Tall and gaunt, with a long, bald head and a pointed nose that almost reminded Didier of a Scandinavian elf from mythology at times.

"We are," Konrad replied.

Didier steeled himself and turned to the woman.

Fraulein Zofija Reiher. A tall, busty, blond, *Übermenschen* woman, built with muscles like a Bavarian peasant, except that he knew her to have competed against men in modern pentathlons. Beautiful, at least on the surface. If you liked them like that.

Both of them were dedicated Nazis. Didier was French, but a fascist like them. He would, however, see the Third Republic overthrown that France might take her rightful place with the Continental Axis that intended to rule the world.

If only the bitch were built like a proper French woman. Didier preferred lean and elegant, rather than top-heavy and athletic. Breasts were supposed to fit in a champagne coupe, rather than a stein.

Fraulein Reiher had forced herself upon him more than he liked since Samarkand, though far less that she might have.

Some middle ground, perhaps, where her sadism could torture him, but not so much that he just shot the two Germans dead and called it good.

A delicate wire to walk, some days.

"But, India?" Didier asked the woman.

At least she was dressed like a high German official. That meant her white shirt fully buttoned, covered with a blazer, and bisected by a black tie.

He'd...*experienced* her in far less. The woman fornicated like she no doubt ran marathons: panting, gasping, and heaving.

It was unfortunate that he needed the two of them. If only for a short period yet.

"India," she confirmed. "Lahore, in the northwest. They did not continue from Samarkand to the northeast, as we had expected, perhaps heading towards Tunguska. In that, we are fortunate that the Soviets did not allow us passage beyond Alma-Ata, else we might never have caught up with them in time."

"But what are they doing?" Didier demanded. "They have nearly a week head start on us. We may never catch up with them as it is."

"Our contacts suggest they have been resting and recuperating in Lahore," Konrad interjected. "Speaking with the local British authorities and contacting the Tibetans about passage. Like us, they have not been granted permission."

"Can we intercept them?" Didier pressed.

At the end of the day, that was what he really needed. To

prevent Shirazi from convincing the Man With No Face to divulge his alien secrets. Or, failing that, to steal them for himself.

Nazi Germany could invade Russia and blunt their strength killing Slavs for all Didier cared. France already had a better empire in Africa with which to eventually challenge the English. And without a world war, the Americans might stupidly withdraw behind their Monroe Doctrine lines again and leave him alone.

"We can," Reiher nodded. "Our spies in Tibet have acquired a set of coordinates that your Persian Princess seems intent upon visiting. Nothing on any maps, but nobody has been able to adequately travel to those valleys anyway."

"Is it Shambala?" he asked, feeling like a fool.

Didier Beauchêne was a man of science, such as Konrad was. Let those damned, foolish Aryans pursue their idiotic metaphysics.

Unless there was something really there.

Reiher had that look in her eyes. That smile. A True Believer. The most dangerous kind, because she would do anything to reach her goals.

Regardless of the number of bodies she might have to pile up in order to get there.

Didier would kill her first, if it came to that. Might even be looking forward to that part.

"It might be, Beauchêne," she replied, licking her lips in an almost orgasmic way.

At least he recognized the look now for what it was.

"How soon until we leave?" he asked.

CHAPTER FIVE

Finn finished packing the last of his gear and various tidbits out of the Condor, including the last couple of pistols that he and Hans had hidden here and there against surprises. They even had those four .303 rifles they'd originally picked up from Magdy back in Cairo, plus various things they'd stolen from Italians, Egyptians, and Soviets along the way.

He still preferred his old Colt Officers Model 1911. Those little 9mm Parabellums everyone in Europe used had a tendency to go right through a man without killing him. A .45 ACP didn't do that.

And you still could just wound a fellow if you had to. And knew what you were doing. That nasty French fellow with all the knives, for instance.

He'd be glad to eventually get rid of the German uniforms Zareen had gotten them for Cyrenaica, though he supposed that something like that would have to wait until they were done in Tibet.

Asher was nearby. Everyone else was hauling boxes to the truck. Finn walked close to the robot.

"What's really there?" Finn asked.

Not like they hadn't had this conversation previously, but nothing had come of it.

Today, they were looking at that wall of mountain and about to surmount it.

For good or ill.

"Honestly, Finn, I do not know," the man replied. Robot. Fellow.

"Guesses?" Finn tried.

"My mission was secret and illegal, as you know, so we could not ask the authorities what resources they might have previously cached on Earth," Asher said. "And I was not entirely prepared to be delivered in the manner that I was."

They shared a grim chuckle. Something had gone wrong with their space plane and it had slammed into a cliff face under power. Everyone aboard burned to a crisp. One exploration robot stripped of his camouflage and left forlorn.

Twenty years later, inquisitive humans had pieced together the man's secrets and tracked him to the slums of Cairo. Then all hell had broken loose.

Finn would have liked to say he would've preferred to have missed it, but he'd be lying.

He felt more alive today than he had since the Great War had ended, bored out of his skull flying back and forth from Rome to Abyssinia, hauling passengers, cargo, and mail.

"It is my hope, from clues I may be misinterpreting on the map, that there exists a base of some sort there," Asher said.

"Isn't that bad, though?" Finn pressed. "I mean, if there is, are there any of those Durren folks you talked about?"

"Perhaps," Asher nodded. "However, we cannot know until we get there."

"But won't they dismantle you if they catch you?" Finn asked. "I'd hate to think that we came all this way just to get you killed."

"I am not alive, Finn," Asher said. "Not as you consider it. I have often considered that I might have been better off walking out into the middle of the ocean and hiding, shutting myself down entirely. At least until the next Durren ship came and scanned for signals. Then they would extricate me and learn everything I knew."

"So you can't hide from them?" Finn asked.

"Indeed, my friend," Asher agreed. "Thus, all I can do is gather more and more data for them. Hopefully, they will eventually turn it into information."

"We're still too dangerous for folks to show up out there and say hello," Finn said.

"Acknowledged," Asher confirmed. "But not all of you are rapacious, bloodthirsty beasts."

The mask wouldn't let him smile, but Finn could hear it in his voice.

"Enough are," Finn said. "A whole lot, when you get right down to it."

"Perhaps," Asher shrugged. "At the same time, I have a duty to continue my studies. Especially if another such war intrudes."

"Next one will be bigger and uglier," Finn said.

"And not everyone is happy to allow the darker elements of mankind to achieve supremacy," Asher countered.

"I thought your programming prevented you from hurting people," Finn said.

"It does," Asher acknowledged. "But I have been forced to adapt. To work my way around certain ethical restrictions. In that, I might place some of the blame directly at your feet, Finn."

"Me?" he recoiled. "What did I do?"

"Showed this poor robot that being a criminal did not necessarily make one evil," Asher intoned. "You do not follow your own laws, or those of others, but only when you seek outcomes that are on balance better for everyone than the strict letter of the law allows."

"So I'm gonna have a warrant out when your folks get here, too?" Finn laughed.

"It is entirely feasible," Asher noted. "My apologies in advance."

"Hey, they still gotta catch me," Finn said. "Other folks have tried, including at least one ex-wife."

"At least one?" Asher asked, turning fully, voice fanciful with curiosity.

"One I know of," Finn laughed.

"How could one be married more than once and not be aware?" Asher pressed.

"Depends on her," Finn said. "What she tells folks. How drunk I might have been at the time. Maybe whatever documents she might have forged. Not like there isn't a good reason I'm avoiding Montana, Des Moines, and Paris, ya know."

"I see," Asher said.

Finn hadn't talked too much about those sorts of things. Statutes of Limitations, and all that.

And maybe abandoned, barely-divroced ex-wives running around.

He figured Tibet might be far enough some of them stopped looking.

The question was what this team would find when they got there.

Or who.

Still, he was committed. *Cerberus* was gone, apparently making a daily passenger and cargo run in Egypt, at least until someone figured out which plane it was. And how it got there. And who might technically own it out of an Italian bankruptcy court.

Same, the California Condor. Absolutely stolen. Fallen off a truck in Suez. Or a boat. Whatever.

And way too hot for him to keep flying anywhere where Germans or Italians might convince someone to arrest him.

Nope, the Condor was likely headed west to Tokyo in the morning.

And he was headed north.

CHAPTER SIX

Zareen had picked them a hotel on the edge of the new British district in Lahore. The town was still small, but she could see that changing rapidly. Modern medicine and improvements in agriculture meant that families could be larger, without having so many children die young.

Hopefully, India would sort out how to feed and care for all those folks before they overwhelmed their own resources. The British weren't necessarily pleasant when dealing with non-whites in their various colonies.

Nor at home, she could speak from experience, though in her case she'd had money, family, and connections to blunt the worst of it. And the Scots were far more friendly as a people.

She stood on the balcony and looked out over the city as it grew dark, until a knock at the door drew her back inside in time to see Ghada admit the men.

Zareen gestured to the bucket of ice with a bottle of champagne on the sideboard.

"This probably calls for a toast," she told them. "Finn, if you would?"

She moved to the couch and sat. Ghada stayed by the door, dressed as a Westerner, which included a small pistol on her hip.

In addition to the knives hidden about. And her warrior dance training.

Emad sat in the wingback chair. Asher and Hans joined her on the couch. Finn poured glasses and rested them on a tray, delivering with the same sort of delicate precision with which he flew.

Zareen raised her glass.

"Shortly, we will be facing the mountains at the top of the world," she reminded them, and then all took a drink. "Now that the aircraft situation has been settled, we'll need gear and weapons. Supplies and such as Asher has listed."

"We know anything about the Frenchie and his Nazi chums?" Finn asked, standing near to where Emad sat.

"We do not," Zareen shook her head. "However, this being India, and the British not being entirely popular around here, I presume that someone has managed to get word of us to some German embassy or consul. After that, it is a question of how quickly that information gets to Didier, and how quickly they can backtrack from wherever we are. I have hope that they might fall for our original track northeast and deflect them to Tunguska, but we cannot know until we confront them again. Or escape entirely."

"What's at this Tunguska place, anyway?" Finn asked, still sipping champagne.

"In 1908, an explosion at low altitude flattened hundreds of square kilometers of forest," Zareen replied. "It took years for the word to get out, because of how remote and backwards the region is and was, but I am unaware of a crater."

Finn turned to Asher.

"'Nother one of your people?" he asked.

"Unlikely, but not impossible," Asher replied in that proper, English accent he did with this group, adding just a touch of Arabic burr underneath, much how her BBC English frequently came flavored with Scottish. "Similarly, the 1930 Curuçá River event in Brazil, up the headwaters of the Amazon, remains unexplained and almost unknown, save for an article found in the Vatican Library archives, a 1931 issue of *L'Osservatore Romano*, which contained a dispatch from the Franciscan friar Fedele d'Alviano, detailing his interviews with locals. Possibly nothing more than an airbursting meteoric explosion, but my datacore contains no more information on either topic than human records."

Finn grunted and Zareen sympathized. So much that nobody knew, except that she had proof that aliens from another world had visited Earth. One of them sat next to her on this very couch.

And had a map that supposedly showed a Durren base in the Tibetan mountains.

"I have been surprised by Didier and others more times than I care to," Zareen pronounced. "Held at gunpoint and threatened with harm. Finn, you and the others have rescued me, but I wish to remind everyone that our game has grown dangerous. Additionally, we cannot begin to guess how the Durren might respond to our trespassing on one of their bases. I will expect everyone to be armed at all times, including myself."

"Only wounded Bertrand," Finn growled. "You saying you want him dead next time?"

"Finn, how many warnings have we given them to leave us alone?" Zareen countered, noting the way the others bristled.

"More than anybody else I have ever known," Finn confrimed. "Most of them took the warning to heart. Or stopped breathing."

Zareen nodded. Finn had done things during American Prohibition that he was not proud of—and didn't talk about— but she hadn't inquired too closely. It was enough to know he had killed people. As had she, but Zareen didn't talk about that in polite company, either.

Of the group, Hans was probably the most innocent, excluding Asher the robot.

"How soon until we are ready to leave?" she asked.

"Test flight went well," Finn noted. "Hans checked the engines. Still want to run it up to ceiling and see how it performs over some mountains, then pull a full maintenance. Gonna be cold up there."

"I shall see to acquiring cold weather gear, Finn," Asher spoke up. "Things such as Tibetans and Nepalese commonly wear. I find that the British have silly ideas on the topic."

Zareen nodded. British pluck was all well and good, but they would be up in a high, Tibetan valley in the early fall. Cold. Not as brutal as in six months, but not a snowy morning in Glasgow, either.

She turned to Emad. Not an outsider, but outside his comfort zone. A Senussi warlord and cousin to Idris of Cyrenaica, the man who would be king.

He read her inquiring look and nodded.

"Kamchatka after that?" he asked, as a way of conveying to her that he would follow her to the ends of the earth if need be.

She nodded back.

"Perhaps the Amazonian headwaters," she grinned.

Wherever there was more information she could find. Zareen would end colonialism. Send the Italians packing from Libya, then the British from Egypt.

Then everyone from Persia. Everyone.

To do that, she needed advanced technology. Weapons, plain and simple, that would make the Russians leave. And the British. And anyone else.

"Thank you for believing in me," she told the group.

They all nodded back, certain things unspoken even here, where the walls might be thin enough to reveal her secrets.

Zareen rose and toasted with what remained of her champagne.

"Tomorrow, then."

CHAPTER SEVEN

Didier had dragged Bertrand along with him as a bodyguard, rather than subjecting himself to the *Fraulein* this morning. They had fled Alma-Ata as far as Stalinabad—which had once been Dyushambe—once the Soviets had demanded that they leave the nation entirely.

Even their Heinkel needed maintenance, so they had come this far and were taking a day before traveling on.

Stalinabad was a quiet town. It had had its ups and downs, and was currently reeling from being renamed for that idiot in Moscow, but Didier didn't say that too loud. Too many Soviet fanatics around here, to go with local hillmen that didn't like outsiders of any kind.

Thus, Bertrand, handy and happy to kill anyone he perceived as a threat.

And a few that maybe were in the wrong neighborhood this afternoon.

They had gone as far as a coffee shop, heavy with cigarette smoke and glowering looks. Didier kept his modified .25 caliber hand cannon in a pocket, in case he needed to kill several some-ones in a straight line.

Most of the folks in here were westerners by dress, and thus nervous whenever the door opened.

Didier sucked on his cigarette and considered his pet assassin.

"And you have no contacts in southern Asia?" Didier asked.

"There has been no time to even begin," the tall assassin shrugged, then flinched where the American had shot him. The wound had healed.

Physically.

"I grow tired of the *Fraulein*," Didier nodded, quiet. "If we were going anywhere but...*there*, I would suggest she come to an unfortunate accident. Schwarzenberg is a scientist, and the submissive half of that pair, and thus I could control him."

"Fuck her to death?" Bertrand offered with a terrible leer. "Or get her pregnant?"

"I'm not sure the former is possible," Didier countered. "And the latter might simply mean she rides into battle with a child on one hip. That woman is the worst kind of fanatic. You will keep your eyes open for ways that her death could be explained as a terrible accident. Even if you have to hire someone in Kabul or wherever we end up next."

"Not Lahore?" Bertrand asked carefully. Quietly, given the location.

"I cannot imagine that we would do anything but show up after they have left already," Didier grimaced. "I grow tired of chasing the Shirazi woman and her friends all over the damned globe. Plus, we have rough coordinates of where they travel to, from our spies where she is now. It should be close enough to let us find their plane. This time, we might destroy it on the ground before landing, just so they cannot escape us again. You should keep that in mind, Bertrand."

The assassin nodded and sipped at his own coffee. His debts to the American gangster known as Severijns were even greater than Didier's to Zareen Shirazi, as difficult as that might be to imagine.

"Pity the Germans won't take your orders," Bertrand grinned.

"Schwarzenberg will," Didier corrected. "I need him to keep the flight crew enchanted, and to continue drawing support from his network of spies. Once I have Shirazi in my hands, he can join the *Fraulein* in hell. Am I clear?"

"Perfectly," Bertrand's smile grew wide and ugly.

Didier had no doubts that the Germans intended to use him as a hound to tree Zareen Shirazi, that they might steal her secrets themselves.

Didier intended to throw down France's Third Republic and replace it with a fascist one. Rule of the strong. Let the Germans carve themselves off an empire from the lands of the Slavs, as France had her colonies in Africa that were more valuable.

But he needed the Germans for now.

For now.

A shadow at the door caused most of the room to flinch. For the other men, a note of uncontrolled lust as *Fraulein* Reiher entered, dressed in clothing civilian enough to not be a uniform, while tight enough to draw the attention of the fools around the room.

It got worse when she approached his table and immediately sat with a smile on her face. It was a pretty face. Blonde hair. Muscular and athletic like a Polish peasant. Black widow in all the ways that counted.

Didier preferred the Whippet to the St. Bernard.

"*Fraulein*," he offered with a polite nod of his head.

"Konrad sent me to find you, Didier," she smiled at him in possessive, feral, *hungry* way. "The pilots intend to make to Kabul this afternoon, instead of waiting for the morning. Our prey grows restive and we must give chase."

"Excellent news," Didier smiled. And it really was. The alternative was a night in the hotel room where she might come knocking at his door.

Hopefully, they would all be so tired after another flight that he could sleep in peace for once.

Schwarzenberg wouldn't believe that Didier had mistaken her for a burglar and shot her in the darkness. Presumably, the man had already been sucked dry by this vampire and left an empty husk as she sought out a new victim.

Unfortunately, her sadism had alighted on Didier, when Bertrand might have been a match made in hell.

He finished his coffee and stubbed out his cigarette, catching both her and Bertrand off guard.

"Come," he exclaimed. "We must get to the airport immediately!"

They followed him to the door, unable to see the smile on his face.

The *Fraulein*'s time was coming to an end. If he could hold his stomach down long enough.

CHAPTER EIGHT

Asher was not programmed thus, but he had come to understand certain human emotions the Durren had meant him to study. They had not intended him to personalize them.

However, living for twenty years without hope of rescue did give one a good grasp of *forlorn*. And he had spent many of those years living in the slums of Cairo, among the poor and middle classes—such as they were—and had learned the calculus of information exchange in ways that the Durren would grasp.

But *trepidation* was something entirely new.

Never before had he worried about his personal chassis. His mere existence was a crime in the eyes of the Durren. And, he supposed, it was entirely possible that they might find his makers when they arrived at the place his maps suggested a Durren base, hidden in the mountains at the top of the world.

Additionally, he had changed in ways that his original programming was not supposed to allow.

He could harm or injure a human through action. Could visualize hurting someone. Had done so, in the effort to protect another human from being injured in a mugging.

*A.S.H.E.R., Mark **Eight**.*

What would his makers say, to understand that he had grown and changed on this world? Been changed by these people?

In the past, Asher might have walked all night, updating his maps of Cairo with a depth of detail that humans were not emotionally equipped to understand. Lahore was different, mostly because he had not lived here for years, and would thus likely come into conflict with local predators if he roamed.

Muggers, to use the vernacular.

While he could injure them to protect himself and Humanity, staying in his room meant that he was not at risk, which thus prevented him from immediately heading out to do something.

Cause trouble, Finn would have described it.

Asher was going to cause trouble. If there were Durren hiding up there, they would object to humans finding them. Would object to an ASHER unit even existing on this world.

At the same time, he had assiduously listened on the correct frequencies for any Durren signals. Finding none did not mean that there were none here, merely that they hid if they were.

As they should.

It was the niggling fear in the back of his head that distressed him.

The knowledge that the advanced nations of the world had been involved in a major conflagration called the Great War when his original builders had chosen to deliver him to the Egyptian desert. And that a greater one was brewing up today.

Would the Durren return to observe a second Great War in detail?

Worse, would they take the opportunity to deliver a few destabilizing blows intended to reduce Humanity to the bronze or iron age simplicity they had had until quite recently?

And would an ASHER unit allow it?

CHAPTER NINE

Finn studied his maps. Crap, all of them. What he needed was something that could fly stupidly high with a camera and take pictures from above.

That Goddard fellow was probably on the right track. Launch something up to the edge of the atmosphere and look down, mapping everything before it fell to Earth again.

Most of the world was known by now. Folks had even been to Antarctica, from Ernest Shackleton down to Richard E. Byrd today. Folks had gone up the Amazon, though not all over yet. Same as they'd gone into the African interior and met the folks living there. Islands in the Pacific.

Tibet was still *tabula rasa*. A blank slate.

At least to outsiders like him.

Finn would have liked better maps. Asher's showed a particular area about the size of a county, back home in Montana. In an area about three times the size of Montana itself.

Fortunately, he didn't need to get anywhere near Lhasa. Unfortunately, the place he was going, the so-called Northern Plateau, was larger than France. And he'd flown most of France in his time.

Plus, in spite of Zareen's friends calling it the Lakes District, you were as like to encounter fresh water as salt, and he didn't have trees handy he could burn to boil off clean water.

Everything they needed, they'd be hauling in themselves.

At least none of the herders they encountered would mistake any of them for Chinese.

"I'm supposed to be the morose son of a bitch around here," Hans said as he slid into the co-pilot's seat.

"Day's young," Finn fired back at him. "Plotting needs against travel weight and altitude. Figure we're nearly seven hundred miles to our target."

"Good thing that *Sunrise* can travel three to four times that amount, then, isn't it?" Hans countered. "Even at altitude. Or were you thinking we needed to carry a fuel barrel, like we did into Cyrenaica that first time?"

"If they didn't have such a warlord and bandit problem, I'd aim for Khotan, but that's likely to be as bad as Kashgar these days," Finn mused. "Kinda a cultural borderline between the Chinese folks on one side and the Muslims and Turks on the other. Afraid we're gonna end up having to fly all the way back here on one tank of gas, 'less we get sneaky on our way out."

"How sneaky?" Hans asked, leaning in.

"Kathmandu, maybe?" Finn offered. "Don't wanna go out through Lhasa, because they might not appreciate what we did. Not a lot of options headed out towards Mongolia."

"We'll make it work," Hans assured him. "Hell, I'm looking forward to hitching a ride on a spaceship when we meet Asher's people."

He would. Finn rolled his eyes at the big Kraut but understood. Hans liked to read weird *scientifiction* pulp to practice his English. Fixed a man up with some bizarre ideas.

Like alien exploration robots running around?

Finn grinned. He was in the middle of worse.

"Come," Hans said, tugging on his sleeve. "Let us get some

soup and some wine in you. The morning will be along soon enough."

Finn allowed himself to be dragged off.

Hans was right.

They'd be off in the morning.

God help them all.

CHAPTER TEN

Zareen considered saying something pithy and impressive, standing on the runway as they had the newly named *Sunrise* facing its namesake. Finn's joke on a Japanese aircraft. The Land of the Rising Sun.

In the end, as she took a breath, Zareen noticed a staff car approaching in the distance. Not the sort of mad dash that had seen the Italians attempt to cut them off at Benghazi, but something about it didn't feel right.

Finn caught her look and turned.

A silent nod, and both were jogging towards the plane, the others reacting quickly. Asher thought the fastest, but took the longest to board.

About what she would expect from a scholar, when the rest of them were adventurers.

Zareen threw herself into a seat to let Hans by in the tight confines. Emad ended up across the aisle, Asher and Ghada a row back as the seats were arranged like a movie theater.

Finn had the engines turning over quickly and *Sunrise* roaring down the runway, leaving the automobile behind.

"Do we know who that was, back there?" Emad asked over the sound.

"Trouble," Zareen replied, leaving it at that.

Emad nodded. His time as a warlord of a band of Senussis in the Cyrenaican desert had developed those same instincts.

Knowing when to cut and run, lest it catch you.

Sunrise leapt into the sky and began a mad dash, north first before they would arc over to the northeast and into the Lakes Districts of Tibet.

And adventure.

Sunrise could reach two hundred knots, and it felt like Finn had the engines wide open, getting them quickly to altitude from the way the ground fell away below.

She agreed.

Get gone now, as Finn liked to say, referencing his smuggler days in the States.

Fortunately, they were fully loaded. Every spare nook and cranny packed with gear, including the leather and fur outfits they would need if it was exceptionally cold. For now, it was fall. Tropical still below and behind them, so she had hopes that it would be no worse than the Swiss Alps or American Rockies on a similar day.

Still, into yet another unknown.

"Asher," she called, turning. "We have begun. Let us pull out your map and study it again as we start getting closer. It is likely that we will be overhead of our target in a few hours, so we should be prepared."

"Agreed, Zareen," Asher said, withdrawing the folded map from a pocket somewhere in his robes and moving to squat in the aisle.

Ghada climbed over, until the four of them formed a compass rose and spread the map out on the floor of the plane.

Canyons. Lakes. A few villages marked, but with no idea how old the map might be, Zareen couldn't guess if those villages had turned into cities, or be entirely abandoned.

Fortunately, none were particularly close to their destination, so she expected that the only people they would see would likely be herders tending their flocks.

What would they think, if they'd perhaps never seen an airplane before? Possibly never even heard of such a thing, as remote as this area could be?

Finn was flying them to an area that other maps showed as a figure eight of lakes, lying on its side with their valley in the east-ern-most half, just east of a glacier that showed on this map.

Was the glacier still there?

She trusted Finn to get them close, but that assumed that the map itself was an honest representation of current geography and even climate of the region.

It would have to do.

Time was of the essence.

CHAPTER ELEVEN

Finn had gotten out of town and sight as if flying back north. Old Rumrunner trick, to make them think you've gone anywhere other than where you really were headed.

Then he'd turned hard and spun it until he was headed more or less due east. Weren't a lot of passes he trusted, to get him and *Sunrise* into the Tibetan interior, so he was aiming for Rohtang Pass, not far from a place marked as Manali on his maps.

Pass was supposedly around 4,000 meters elevation. Would have been a bit of a problem for the Condor, which really topped out at about 6,500 meters ceiling, but *Sunrise* could get you over 9,000 meters. Enough that he'd be mostly invisible from the ground, even over the pass itself.

God only knew what kind of watchers might be sitting up there, relaying radio calls somewhere to complain about English and American adventurers trespassing.

Good thing he was going into the literal middle of nowhere. Even worse than Nebraska.

Beside him, Hans was sketching maps on blank paper, then stopped and muttered a long string of profanities under his breath, yet still loud enough for Finn to hear.

He unbuckled and stood up.

"I am a dumbass," Hans announced.

"Not arguing," Finn called. "What are we talking about?"

He liked the dark glower that came over Hans's face, followed by a quick eyeroll.

"Be right back," Hans said, then disappeared aft.

A few moments later, Asher appeared, taking the copilot seat while Hans went into the radio operator's spot. Headphones got put on, because while the robot could hear him over the engines, Asher would have to yell.

"Okay, Hans, I have joined you," Asher said calmly, head rotated all the way backwards like an owl.

Really weird to see.

"I was starting to map the terrain for our return," Hans said over the intercom. "It dawns on me that you could do a much better job of it, and faster."

"You are correct," Asher noted, then jolted as if surprised. "Oh, I could map western Tibet for you. For anyone desiring such maps, I suppose."

"Just the little lady for now," Finn corrected. "Maybe we'll mail copies to the authorities in Lhasa at some point, just so they have them. Don't rightly see where the Brits in India need to know. Or the Russians, ya know?"

Asher's head rotated to a more normal spot, scowling at him with that enameled mask. Then a nod.

"Because that would allow military forces to more easily invade, yes," Asher realized.

"Especially as they can fly over ground troops," Finn agreed. "Drop someone in the rear and maybe keep them resupplied. Can't hold against an army, but you could surprise someone and that's a good way to rout them. That German guy, Rommel, talked about lightning warfare and rapid maneuver into somebody's rear as a way of beating them. Aircraft make it even easier."

"Would people go to war over a place like Tibet?" Asher asked.

Finn shrugged.

"People do stupid shit for stupid reasons," he replied. "The Chinese like to claim Tibet. The Brits would probably love to add it to their possessions in India and the south. You got the Soviets on the north side, presumably looking to expand any way they can, especially with the Germans on their western front, breathing heavy. There's a reason we're still marked Red on all those Durren maps, you know."

"It is unfortunate that I must agree with you, Finn," Asher said.

At the same time, the robot picked up Hans's notebook and began mapping. Almost as good as you could get from a mapbook, but Finn supposed that Asher would be able to memorize all this and put it on a larger piece of paper later. He'd said something about having a map of Cairo at a level of detail that would probably frighten folks.

Finn nodded and watched the robot work. This would be a hell of a lot easier with skymaps, when he needed to backtrack later.

Be even better if they did go out a different direction and Asher could map that.

Hell, with the flight ceiling on *Sunrise*, maybe they needed to haul Asher all over the world and let him make precise maps. Better than anything anyone had today.

Except that maybe that would make invasions easier.

Finn reconsidered and decided that he didn't really trust anybody but Zareen with that sort of thing.

In the distance, the Himalayan mountains beckoned.

CHAPTER TWELVE

Didier studied the rolling terrain from out of one of the tiny windows that had been added when the aircraft had been converted from a bomber to a civilian transport.

And, he had to admit, the Germans were more advanced than his own countrymen when it came to technology.

Part of that, he knew, was the Spanish Civil War, where the Condor Legion fought. German "mercenaries" who were simply army units transferred to help the Nationalists crush the communists. Along the way, they had begun sprinting forward in terms of industrial development.

Time spent on warfare instead of seducing pretty girls in cabarets.

Thus, the Third Republic would fall at some point. Too many Frenchmen still lounging on the glories of Bonaparte, after they had lost several wars to the Germans and British over the last century.

He kept his face focused on the view as a body slid into the seat next to him.

Too close. Too warm.

Too touchy.

"Something interesting below, Didier?" *Fraulein* Reiher

asked over the roaring hum of the engines, leaning in to press one ample breast into his arm as she breathed on his ear.

Here, you nymphomaniac demon? Right here, in the back of the aircraft, in front of Konrad and Bertrand? Is there any limit to your debaucheries?

But he didn't say that. Didn't even think it too loudly. Simply pasted a neutral smile on his face, then turned inward on her, until they ended up almost nose to nose. He even leaned a little into the woman as she backed away.

Oh, don't like that, do you?

He let a hint of triumph into his smile. She was a woman who pushed, because most men gave ground. Manners, for many. Fear, from others.

Didier wondered if he'd just unlocked the puzzle of her being.

She didn't like it when someone simply pushed back without otherwise reacting.

"Thinking about this situation," he offered ambiguously. "About Tibet. It would, on the surface of things, have no connection to the Man With No Face. Nor to Egypt, or even distant Tunguska. I wonder if it is a trap."

Didier found himself leaning into the woman as she leaned away, so he relaxed into his seat again, allowing a wider no-mans-land to develop between them.

For now.

"A trap?" she asked, eyes still a little wary, since he hadn't recoiled away from her as she'd apparently been expecting. Like every time before.

Didier wondered what reception he might get if he were to knock on *her* door tonight. Or perhaps her tent, as they were headed into a desolate wilderness.

What was she like, if the roles suddenly reversed?

Could *femme fatales* know disquiet?

His smile grew.

"They fled Egypt for the northeast," Didier replied.

"Samarkand in Soviet Central Asia. We had thought that they fled onward, as though to Tunguska, but now we know that they circled back, clear around the Tibetan plateau through Afghanistan, into British India."

She nodded, recovering her poise slowly.

"What could there possibly be in northern Tibet that is worth all this effort?" he asked. "I find myself wondering if this is a ploy. A way to get us isolated from any assistance, that they might destroy us."

"They had their chance in Samarkand, Beauchêne," she countered.

"And they used machine guns on your car to kill your driver after you opened fire on them," he reminded the woman. "You and Konrad were both ejected from the vehicle, though you fell safely. The flight crew was captured but not harmed. Thus, a pattern of behavior, where Zareen Shirazi and I have been dancing, but never to lethality, even when it was perhaps warranted. Even the American gangster supposedly only wounded Bertrand when he shot my assassin."

"And?"

"At what point would they tire of this game, and decide to ambush and kill us, *Fraulein*?" he growled.

By herself, Didier doubted that the woman would. She had never used lethal force before. Then he amended himself to *yet*, uncertain with a few instances that had been ambivalent at best. And Ghada Attar was at least as dangerous as Bertrand.

It was the addition of Severijns and Emad al-Sadri, both warriors from warlike cultures.

That might tip the scale.

Again, the probabilities were low, but Didier wanted to plant a seed. Make her nervous. Make Konrad nervous.

Make all the Germans nervous, in case the *Fraulein accidentally* ended up dead later.

He would make sure Shirazi took the blame.

"What would you suggest?" Reiher asked.

"When we see the stolen Heinkel, perhaps we should destroy it from the air," Didier suggested. "This aircraft is armed. Then we find a place to land, refuel the tanks from the barrels stored aboard, then set off after them, certain that this flight crew is prepared to kill Shirazi and her associates when they appear, while we go after them with the same murderous intent."

"Murderous, Beauchêne?"

"I also tire of the game, *Fraulein*," he growled at her over the engines. "It has gone on long enough, and we should end it. Kill Shirazi and her friends. Capture the Man With No Face and force him to divulge his secrets. Take that information back to a civilized land, where we can take advantage of it. Did you have something else in mind?"

He watched her eyes as she spun ideas, discarded lies, and reevaluated plans quickly.

If nothing else, the woman was exceptionally intelligent. And, he would grant, beautiful.

Too muscular by half for him. And noisy in bed in bad ways.

But not stupid.

And he found now that she had buttons he could push. Carefully, because he didn't want her to realize it too quickly, but maybe, just maybe, he could turn the tables on this woman, as she had done to him.

Didier was tired of coming out on the losing side to the women in his life, even if they tended to be exceptional women.

This time, he intended to win.

CHAPTER THIRTEEN

Asher gave thought to Finn's words as he mapped the western Tibetan mountains and plateaus. For all that he liked certain humans, and had come to see himself as something of a protector of the species against future Durren interference, there was something to be said for the fact that the knowledge he had assembled could be used for evil purposes.

Maps, for invaders. Social and Urban Geography, for Durren scientists who might take his findings and use them to tip this world culture and civilization backwards over into that place they had just emerged from...

He had read Locke and Hobbes. Lao Tzu and the Buddha. A variety of sacred texts from many cultures. Asher supposed that he really did understand this species as well as any alien might, and better than many humans probably did, with their own blinders limiting their ability.

Even the American politician Jefferson had spoken powerful words about liberty and equality, then fallen well short in his personal behavior. As many did.

It was an interesting way to consider humans, both as individuals as well as a species. And far beyond the limits of his original programming, but Asher had never been intended to remain on Earth this long. He would have been recovered after no more than five years, to take what he had learned for his outlaw sociologists, that they could make better A.S.H.E.R units for the future.

Instead, they had all died in the Cyrenaican desert, leaving him alone.

Asher was not alone today, but he had to weigh far greater things. The man next to him was a criminal by his own admission, and yet Asher would rate Finnley Severijns as one of the good guys.

Emad al-Sadri was a rebel warlord from the deep deserts, but he merely wanted to evict the Italians that Cyrenaica might become a free nation.

Zareen Shirazi...

Asher understood that her goals would end up destabilizing large portions of this world. Driving the British out of Persia. And forcing the Soviet Union to withdraw.

And keeping everyone else at a distance, where the Shia minority sect of Islam might know their own safe homeland, surrounded on all sides by Sunni and infidels, at least as they might measure such things.

Persia, free of interference. Enforced at the end of a gun, at that.

And Asher intended to help.

He opened a new file for his musings and categorized things that would allow him to help colonies of the European powers throw off their chains, in the means of protecting them, as Asher had once protected an older human male in the process of being mugged by a younger one.

When had he become a hero?

Asher let his hands work on the maps, while his mind broke through yet another set of behavioral boundaries and considered how he might make Earth a better—safer—place for everyone.

CHAPTER FOURTEEN

Finn had never been here, but Asher had one hell of a hand for mapping things.

They were coming out of the southwest, with the sun on his right. Big glacier on his left. Salt pan kind of valley in front of him, draining down to a lake he assumed was going to be too nasty to drink.

Ridge of mountains just north of that lake, rippled on the back side like a gator half down in the water with the way the shadows played. Kinda nifty to look at, but reminded him that things might be far more dangerous than they appeared, once he got on the ground.

Kinda like it had been landing at Gabal El Uweinat, only to be snuck up on by Emad and a bunch of his kinfolk.

Landing here wouldn't be all that different, either, though he had lots more fuel this time.

Finn put things into a slow, left-handed orbit, then looked over at Asher.

"We're here," he announced in a relaxed voice.

Finn was, at the end of the day, just the driver. Zareen and Asher were the motivators.

Asher looked up from his mapping and tapped a control on

the dash. They hadn't gotten around to painting over the Japanese characters with English or German yet, so about half of what was going on eluded him.

Might have to learn to read Japanese at some point. Although, if he was going to keep working for Zareen, Finn could see speaking it. Wasn't like he didn't have a pretty good tutor sitting next to him.

"The temperature on the ground should be roughly eight degrees," Asher announced.

Finn shivered, then remembered to convert to metric. About forty-five out there. Cool, but not bitter. Sun was out and there hadn't been much wind, so his flannel union suit for flying and a jacket for walking around. Probably dig out that big yak leather thing Asher had gotten anyway, just because it would get stupid cold at night.

He'd flown into Las Vegas a few times.

Asher pointed to a spot on his new map, then out into the distance.

Not all that far from the lake that looked like a salt pan from here. Probably spring melt filled it, then summer evaporated it off.

"There is a small canyon we can walk up from the level ground below," Asher said. "Then turn to the right when we get halfway and into the little side canyon above. There should be a portal we can access."

Finn keyed the microphone aft.

"Zareen, can you and Hans switch places for a bit?" he asked. "I think we're ready to land. Slightly concerned about bandits."

Hans laughed. That bandit was aft, sitting next to Zareen.

She appeared a moment later. Hans gestured her to lean over his shoulder and stayed put. Everyone had joined her.

"If we land here, we walk up this place," Finn said. "I'm going to drop down on the next pass and buzz it low enough that Asher might see something out the left side. All of you watch left as well. Everyone hold on."

Like his California Condor, and *Cerberus* before it, *Sunrise* seemed to understand when he needed a smooth flight, because they came out of a tight turn above the glacier itself and dropped down below the level of the hills on either side. Usually, you got a lot of wind in here, but the breeze was into his face and *Sunrise* took to it like a salmon climbing a stream to spawn.

Finn was too busy flying in tight terrain to watch anything, so he relied on the others. Must have been good, because Ghada yelled something aft. The others chimed in.

Finn concentrated on not hitting anything. Dangerous flying, even going almost perfectly straight, but not as risky as crop-dusting, and he'd done some of that in his time, too. Mostly he'd been flying in and out of places too fast for the cops or other mobs to react. Get in, get down, get gone.

He emerged from the mouth of the canyon and over another salt pan pond, already dry. *Sunrise* was low, but he needed to baseline this before he got crazy, because this aircraft wasn't built with the high ground clearance *Cerberus* had had.

Still, old wash turned smooth. Probably ground down by glaciers and weather, and nobody up here was farming it. Not a billiards table, but not all that bad either.

He swooped up and away, turning clockwise this time.

"Everyone get in a chair and get buckled," he yelled, ignoring them after that as he juggled vectors in his head.

Temperature. Weather. Climate. Desert. Cold. Yak herders.

Asher and Hans swapped places, with the big Kraut putting his hands on the controls but not doing anything yet.

Prepared, because rough field landing in the middle of nowhere, without anybody walking it first, was one of the dumbest things in the world for a pilot to do.

Sunrise came around and got lined up.

"Hans, hopping over this shoulder then dropping down

hard and fast," Finn said. "Almost stalling things when I do, but if I yell, I want you to put the throttles to the stops to give me as much power as we can get while I pull on the stick and you release the flaps."

"Roger that," Hans said, suddenly deadly serious copilot.

Always a risk, but you might fall over getting out of bed and crack your skull on a dresser.

And *Sunrise* was listening, too, because he came over that ridge like a hawk falling on a sleeping pigeon. Finn actually had to flatten his dive a little because the stall was so utterly perfect.

One hell of an airplane at low elevation, but he supposed that anything designed to launch torpedoes at battleships had to be.

Gear down. Nose flat. Hawk falling out of the sky.

Flat terrain. No trees. No herders.

No yaks.

Touchdown.

Hard-packed, like he'd just known, even with all the silt that a glacier will wash down the mountain. Nowhere to go, so it baked in on top of permafrost.

Like landing on a frozen lake, except he had grip with the wheels.

Finn throttled down hard almost as soon as *Sunrise* touched, then rolled smooth as silk across the packed dirt towards the big salt pan lake in the distance. Several miles of space over there, but he didn't necessarily want to use it.

Still, rather than stop right here, he let the plane roll for a bit. Test everything while he was in a good spot, then get to a point where he could either run back up this big wadi to take off, or roll over there and take off across the lake, depending on the wind.

His soul knew that the winds were going to come at him from the west, so he'd been headed uphill when he went to leave.

But that was later.

"We're here," Finn said as he shut down the engines.

CHAPTER FIFTEEN

Zareen wanted to yell for joy, but kept herself composed. Several years of research and various adventures, trying to establish that aliens had come to Earth, and she was on the verge of being able to prove it.

Or not, as she might have to take this particular secret to her grave.

In that, she and Didier did share a trait.

She turned to Ghada, also vibrating with mad energy, but Ghada had been with her as a friend, protector, and confidante for many years. She understood the scope.

"Stairs," Ghada said simply. "Carved into the face of the rock in such a way that I think they might be invisible from below."

Zareen nodded. She'd wondered how the locals might have missed it.

At the same time, it was not far from the base of the glacier, and she supposed that this was an inhospitable place at the best of times.

Zareen unbuckled and rose. She headed forward to where Finn and Hans had landed them, Asher still seated nearby.

"How far?" she asked.

"Roughly one point two miles to the mouth of the canyon," Asher spoke first, busy mapping in great detail in a journal without looking down. "Slightly longer than four miles up the canyon to the place Ghada spotted that I take to be our entrance. The weather is cool but pleasant, and there are no storms currently scheduled for this region, based on what we saw in Lahore."

She nodded. All the details she needed in order to make her decision, because all of these men automatically deferred to her to make them.

"Can we disable the plane and leave it here, then move up the canyon and establish a partial base camp?" she asked.

Egypt was hot and dry. You needed water and shade more than anything. Here, it was cold, so you needed more layers. And dry, because you could not trust any standing water.

Ice might be acceptable. Might. Still better to melt it then boil it off in a condenser she had acquired for the task.

Useful, for as long as they had fuel for the Coleman stove. Or could adapt something from *Sunrise*'s fuel tanks.

Finn turned to Hans. The German mechanic nodded.

"Easy enough to do something to the distributor that it won't turn over until we get back," the man rumbled. "You expecting trouble?"

"No," Zareen said. "But this aircraft represents our only means of departure later. I'd like nobody to happen along and steal it while we're busy, and it will be too cold for Hans to sleep in the plane, so he will join us forward."

Nods. Acceptance of her orders.

How many women ever got to say that?

"Five miles hike, slightly uphill," Emad noted. "Cold weather. We can pack tents, but those are heavy."

"I can carry a tent without assistance," Asher reminded them. "And one of the large jerry cans of water. I might suggest we only take the one tent, and everyone sleep in a jumble like cats, at least for tonight. Tomorrow, we can determine if we need the other tent or more supplies. Additionally, I can spend the night ferrying equipment, once someone gives me a priority list."

Zareen blinked, then nodded.

In her mind, he was another person. Another human, or close enough.

She tended to forget that he did not need sleep. Could carry heavy loads without tiring.

Could make this so much easier, because his physical abilities were so much more than anybody else.

"Yes," she said simply. "Emad, you sort that part out, as we're in a cold desert here and your expertise will be invaluable. I'll start sorting my gear with Ghada."

The men nodded and everyone trooped aft. Ghada had a pair of backpacks for them already set and ready to go, along with a belt that had a canteen and pouches for gear.

And her Mauser Broomhandle 7.63mm on a strap over her shoulder.

Outside, the weather was chilly, but the wind was mostly calm. A good day for an Alpine hike, though they were much higher.

As she watched, the men began sorting duties, with Hans moving to disable both engines. A pile of gear got divided out, then part of it put back.

What they could carry now, against what Asher would spend the evening retrieving for them on tireless, robotic legs.

She watched Finn wind his watch. Almost a nervous habit, but one she had come to understand was his way of acknowledging when things were about to get serious. Asher spoke a number and all of them set their timepieces against that. She didn't wear a watch, but supposed that an adventuress might need such a thing.

Later, after she got down off of this mountain.

Quickly enough, they were sorted out and bundled up. Not heavy coats, though Finn had put his on. She could see a faint sheen of perspiration on his brow, but he wore many layers and the cold later would have to get through them.

"I shall lead," Emad announced.

Like Finn and Hans, he had one of those British .303 rifles they had originally purchased from an arms smuggler in Cairo named Magdy. Ghada had the fourth. Everyone but Asher also had pistols where they could get to them quickly, either on a hip or under a coat in Finn's case.

The path was obvious, watching the way spring melt runoff had carved the valley above and laid out this valley floor, with the only tracks being where *Sunrise* carved its furrows on landing.

Zareen took a deep breath and settled things as Emad began to walk.

CHAPTER SIXTEEN

Emad was back on Cyrenaica, on a bitterly cold, full moon night, stalking Italian invaders intent on ravaging his homeland and killing his relatives. His friends. Total strangers who had had the audacity to live there when the Italians decided that they needed an empire and began carving it out of the lives of the folks they found.

He couldn't kill all the Italians in the world, but he shared with Zareen the dream to crush their imperial dreams and see them home and not bothering anyone.

Or killing the ones who refused.

Thus, his mind dropped down into that deadly place, where every sound might be a soldier about to stand up and open fire from behind a rock. Every rock in the path might hide a mine, set to explode and kill him and all his friends.

Emad stalked the plateau like the desert back home, ten meters out front of the others and constantly watching for anything that would necessitate the British rifle in his hands coming up for the first, snap, shot. It was a bolt action with eleven rounds. Ten in the magazine plus one he had hand loaded, in case he needed one more.

With any luck, no shots would be needed at all, because

there was nothing around here. Nobody. Not even wild animals, because the high desert was too *everything* for many to survive.

Those that did would be dangerous, but Emad al-Sadri was far more dangerous.

He had even considered attaching the spike bayonet for this stalk, but decided against it.

For now.

The first mile was easy. Almost perfectly flat, with just the slightest incline before him. From here, the walls of the mountains rose, channeling him into a narrow canyon where spring waters would run off and fill this basin.

It was fortunate, then, that they had come in fall.

He had a rough spot marked in his head where Ghada had seen something. His angle had been wrong, but Emad had marked the terrain and the mountain itself.

He paused.

Knelt on the smooth, sandy soil.

Went ahead and pulled out the bayonet and stuck it into the ground, just test the soil. Ice, not too deep below, from the way it stopped. Silty and packed like the deep desert above that.

"We will leave tracks," he reminded the others, looking back at his own and noting the path.

Until rain or wind came along, anyone finding *Sunrise* would know exactly where they had gone to.

Back home, there were ways to obscure things. A cloak or blanket, filled with sand and dragged behind you to leave a different kind of mark.

A tracker of sufficient skill would be able to see things, but perhaps only that someone had traveled, rather than details of their number and gender.

Had Finn or Asher seen anyone, Emad would grow concerned, but this region was supposedly only inhabited by herders in villages, and they had seen no herds.

Hopefully, no Tibetans had seen or heard them fly over.

Satisfied, Emad put the bayonet away and rose.

Continued his stalk, eyes always up for someone on a cliff or hilltop suddenly appearing, with trouble in their eyes.

The second one might prove a problem, because he would shoot the first one dead as soon as they pointed a weapon at Zareen.

And, he supposed, Finn might get the second, almost as quickly.

Emad had seen his reflexes in action. And his skill with a gun.

It was good.

He continued to stalk.

CHAPTER SEVENTEEN

Because she normally worked as a bodyguard, Ghada would normally dress in Persian robes.

Here, she wore the garments of an adventurer, same as Zareen did, and looked like another one of them.

She even let Emad lead, because he did have more experience with this sort of terrain than she, however barely, though she would not tell him that. Instead, Ghada focused on the spot she had seen as she walked, envisioning how it would appear from below, to a simple herder following yaks and other creatures from plant to plant.

There were not many things for a yak to eat up here. Low brushes that looked more woody than green. Hardy enough to survive and adapted to the cold and dry air.

"Hold," she called at one point as they got close, but not too close.

Guns came up and the men all faced outwards, but Ghada remained locked on the thing that she had seen.

"Asher, how good are your eyes?" she asked, never looking away.

"Better than yours," he said simply.

She supposed so, given that they were electronic and would never grow old and dim. Never need lenses. Never fail him.

She pointed an arm and a finger.

"Look there," she said simply.

He came around behind her and squatted enough to use her arm like a rifle site. He had no breath, which always caught her off-guard, thinking that a man had come up.

"Yes," he agreed. "A cunning way to hide it. Should I scout ahead and confirm?"

Ghada turned to Zareen with a questioning look. She knew exactly where it was now. Asher did as well, so they would not miss it when they got closer.

"What did you see?" Zareen asked them.

"A staircase, carved into the face of stone sideways," Ghada nodded. "It appears to have been set back in such a way that from directly below all you would see is the edge of a ridgeline running up. Nothing made by man."

"As we surmised," Zareen nodded back. "It is tempting to do so, but we should not separate the party. Let me know when we get close enough that we can set things down and establish our base camp. As much as I would like to see, it can wait until tomorrow if need be. We'll need to be settled and warm tonight."

Ghada agreed. She had spoken merely because the robot explorer could move quickly when he needed to, and not be harmed by many things.

Unfortunately, most of the ones that could threaten Asher were likely to be found inside that mountain.

She concentrated on memorizing the exact spot, then nodded for Emad to continue.

She had her target.

Soon, they would walk up those steps and see what Asher's creators had done.

CHAPTER EIGHTEEN

Finn was trailing like a wingman, watching the corners while Emad had the front. Nothing jumped out and tried to get them. Probably would have died in a hail of angry bullets if it had, and the critters running around here had all decided that today was a good day to stay in their dens and sleep.

He was okay with that.

Hell of a hike, but they were done now. Asher and Ghada had conferred and marked a little dry wadi that was apparently more than it let on, because they moved a bit upstream of it and were setting the tent and gear.

Asher had paused, rotating his head in place like a damned owl, then nodded.

"I do not detect any sounds that do not belong in this milieu," he said.

Took Finn a second to translate that into English. Fellow always used five-dollar words in casual conversation.

Finn studied the sky. Still clear, with a few clouds scudding by in a way that said high pressure for a few days, then a storm front behind that.

Maybe the start of the winter monsoon season. Or whatever they got this far north in the Himalayan rain shadow.

Hopefully, they'd be long gone by then and back down in the lowlands somewhere.

Or Hans might get his chance to ride in a spaceship.

"Thoughts?" Zareen asked, sliding close.

"Good enough here," Finn replied. "Tent about there, in case we do get any sort of rain. Dunno about flash floods up here, but this spot is high enough to buy us time in anything less. Sun will be behind the mountains in another hour and we'll be in the shade, so this is probably about as far as we should push today."

"Agreed," she said. "Asher, could you start back to get more gear now? We'll get the tent set up and get ready for night."

"As you wish, Zareen," Asher said, immediately putting down his heavy gear and starting down the valley at a fast jog that made Finn tired just watching.

But the man really was a machine. Gotta remember that.

Finn moved over then he and Hans started unrolling the tent. Pegs were in the middle, along with a couple of nifty aluminum poles that would keep the peak up. Comfortable for two, it would be a bit crammed with five. And warm, like puppies in a pile.

Might be necessary when the temperature dropped below freezing.

And the cloth was good oilskin. A little stinky, but rain-proof against anything short of a hurricane or Noah's flood.

They hadn't brought the campaign chairs on this run, so everybody had sleeping bags that had damned sure come a long ways from the cowboy bedrolls he'd had as a kid. Light and quilted. Pretty damned warm, too. Couple of blankets to throw over that when Asher returned and folks would be all toasty.

Best part, nobody had to stay out in the cold keeping watch and risking frostbite. Asher would have that covered for them.

For now, they got things unrolled, unfolded, and stashed in the tent. Had food for tonight and a Coleman stove to warm some soup and coffee in the morning.

Not exactly the opposite of sleeping in a hammock under *Cerberus*'s wing, but certainly not entirely roughing it, either.

They got things set up about the time Asher returned with his first load. Hans was cooking. Emad had taken a watch. Finn was standing around.

"What do you think we'll find up there?" Zareen asked, stepping close enough to keep her voice low.

"Stairs already tell me that someone has been up there," Finn replied. "Figure they've carved themselves a den in there like a bear. Dunno how big, but if they went to all this effort, on top of coming here in the first place, I'd guess something big enough to matter. Flight base, maybe, like the Army Air Corp is doing?"

"Or an aircraft carrier?" she pressed.

"Doubt it," Finn countered. "According to Asher, the ship that brought him to Earth was only about three times the size of the Condor, though it was more like a flattened egg than a snake with wings. Figure they can travel in their own Condor or *Sunrise*, so they don't necessarily need something utterly huge. Might have them, but remember, these folks were outlaw scientists. Kinda like someone else I know."

It was fun, watching the woman blush. Hard to do, but every once in a while he found a way.

After all, if he couldn't tease his niece, who could?

Finn grinned. She smiled after a moment.

"I find myself nervous," she admitted quietly. "After all these years, to be on the precipice."

"Understand," Finn nodded. "Lots of folks have spent a lot of time and money getting here. And you're going to be the first human to see some of these things, I'd wager."

She nodded back, grateful. Finn smiled.

"Food is ready," Hans announced.

Sounded like a good break. Eat, then go to bed early, because they'd be up early to fix some breakfast.

Then commit some casual burglary.

CHAPTER NINETEEN

Zareen had hardly slept, but that hadn't surprised her. And she had youth on her side, to let her push through in ways that the others would tire first.

Possibly, she amended herself, considering that Ghada was barely older, while Finn, Emad, and Hans seemed to be forged of far sterner stuff than most men she had ever known.

Ghada had risen early and was making a quick bread more like an American flapjack than anything, but they lacked a proper oven, and warmth had seemed to be an important ingredient at this elevation.

Coffee, because coffee, though she had been raised on tea in both cultures.

Today needed that extra grinding edge of bitterness, it felt.

Asher had indeed retrieved a great deal of gear, in case they needed to stay in this location for several days, while perhaps penetrating the facility and withdrawing, time and again as they sought out its secrets.

And very little here that could not be abandoned, if they somehow awakened whatever dread genie they might find inside the place and ended up running for their lives.

Breakfast went quickly. They had established a latrine off to one side, downhill and downwind.

Everyone, it seemed, was prepared, even as the sun was just lightening things enough to be able to see in this canyon.

They had flashlights. And a Coleman lantern if they needed it. Backpacks. Rope. Tools.

Guns.

Zareen took a deep breath to center her mind, then nodded to Ghada.

She hadn't followed the conversation, but Ghada had taken it upon herself to lead this morning, and the men had acquiesced. Asher was at the rear, because he did not have the knack for walking silently.

Quiet. Almost as quiet as Zareen. The others—somehow including Hans—moved as ghosts.

Ghada took them up that little side wash. Over rocks and steps that would probably be a beautiful waterfall, if you caught it at the right moment in summer. After the spring floods, before everything dried out finally.

It did not take long to find the staircase. Zareen paused to examine the steps themselves, then stood and turned to Asher.

"How tall is the average Durren?" she asked simply.

"Perhaps the same height as Hans," he replied. "With a build more like Finn."

Broad and strong then. And tall, as Hans was about six foot three.

Dangerous in person, then. But still mortal, as their plane crash had killed all the others while destroying Asher's disguise.

She nodded. The staircase was scaled to humans. Or Durren, perhaps.

Zareen nodded for Ghada to begin her ascent.

CHAPTER TWENTY

Ghada flowed up the stairs, noting that they had been carved with the slightest incline, so that water flowing would carry away any dirt that had accumulated.

And done so long enough ago that time and entropy had begun to wear the treads down.

How many centuries would that take?

She considered Asher's comment that he had been programmed to speak and read a number of languages that no longer existed, their entire cultures having disappeared.

And she didn't think that was limited to the Catholics or the Han conquering various places and erasing the natives.

Time itself had rendered some people mute, save that Asher could read their words.

Did he have memories of the lands before the Prophet (PBUH) had come? When the Zoroastrians had been dominant?

How much of Persia's ancient history did he know?

The Mistress was all about the present and the future, but Ghada found herself wondering how much of Persia's ancient glories might be available if she asked him.

Food for thought.

For now, she flowed up the stairs like water occasionally flowed down, leaving no mark and making no sound.

The Durren were not superhuman. She realized that they had carved the stone in such a way as to leave landings about every sixty steps going up. As if needing to rest on their climb.

Several such landings, but she took to pausing at each one to understand the construction.

And because her paranoia saw each as a good place to establish traps, were one of a mind.

The fourth pause was different somehow. Each had been similar enough, but something caught her eye.

"Asher," she murmured, knowing that he was listening.

The man stepped close as Ghada studied the rock face itself. Something was off, but she could not place it.

The others spread out, Emad going up several steps and Finn down, to clear the landing itself in case...something.

"What do you see, Ghada?" Asher asked as he came up beside her.

"This feels false," she replied.

"False?"

Ghada drew one of her many knives and stepped right up, using the pommel to tap the stone.

It rang hollow.

Intrigued, she moved to her left and tapped. Stone. Solid. Granite. Mountainous.

Then she shifted across, tapping until she found the tone change. Continuing, she found something that was about two meters wide. Taller than she could reach.

The face had many seams where stone had broken away, but she realized that she was looking at a door, once her mind mapped the hollow parts.

A false metal doorway.

"Interesting," Asher noted, stepping close as well.

Ghada watched him touch the rock in a certain place, then move his hand twice.

A sound thunked through the portal heavy enough that she felt it in her shoes.

"What is it?" Zareen asked.

"Ghada has found a hidden door," Asher said. "The map had hints, but I didn't understand some of those symbols until I realized that they included the code to open the door."

As Ghada watched, the stone began to pivot slowly towards her. She started to step in, but Finn caught her arm.

"Not yet," he said simply. "Let it breathe. Been there a while. Air might have gone all stale."

Ah. Yes. That made perfect sense.

Looking at the door, it was easily fifty centimeters thick. Metal of a kind she could not identify, even when tapping it with her knife.

New to her.

Presumably, some alien alloy of the type the Mistress sought, in order to liberate their homeland.

The faintest breeze kissed her cheeks. It smelled metallic, and industrial, that odd mix of ozone and grease you got when old machines had sat too long.

"Is it a trap?" Emad asked, still watching the rest of the walkway to the top.

"If anything, I would expect that the trap is at the top of the staircase," Asher offered. "A door, obvious and visible, but perhaps merely attached to the stone itself, rather than covering a tunnel inwards."

"Spend all your effort up there and nothing at all to show for it?" Finn asked.

Ghada nodded at the cruelty of such a trick. To come this far and yet fail at the end.

She looked inside. A tunnel, rounded and smoothed, with a flat floor.

Bored perfectly circular, then a walking surface added? It had that feel, as the floor was a slightly different shade of gray/orange stone.

The breeze faded. She glanced at Finn and he nodded, so Ghada took the first step, to the edge of the threshold.

If it was a trap, better that it kill her, as each of the others were far more valuable. And Zareen could return to the highlands for her sisters, cousins, or nieces, when she needed a new protector.

Nothing jumped out.

Ghada paused, then stepped inside.

Lights came up, paired in long strips at where the corners overhead would be, if this was square. And she didn't see any light fixture. It was as if the stone itself glowed.

Or was it all some magical form of alien concrete, embedded with their various devices?

Ghada took several more steps in, turning to look at the inside of the door. It had some alien writing she could not begin to understand. Closer to ancient Egyptian or Chinese than anything else she could think of.

Fortunate, then, that Asher read it. She could see convincing him to teach her. It appeared to be extremely dense with information, so unlike written Persian, which tended to the flowery.

Ghada exited and noted the way the others relaxed.

"So far, so good," she offered. "Should we delve?"

"Indeed, Ghada," Asher nodded. "This would appear to be our avenue of access. Zareen?"

The Mistress took a moment, rotating in place to look above as well as below.

"Yes," she said finally. "We appear to have arrived."

CHAPTER TWENTY-ONE

"We appear to have arrived," the call came over the intercom, rousing Didier from his meditations.

He stirred and leaned to look out the window, noting that the *Fraulein* remained on her side of the aisle doing the same.

"*Was is los?*" she said, loud enough and angry enough that he heard her over the engines.

Didier unbuckled and rose, stepping over and leaning into the woman—*accidentally*—as she had done to him more than once.

Violating her personal space.

Paybacks—a phrase Bertrand had picked up from his American radio dramas—could be a bitch.

Reiher flinched at first contact, then held herself perfectly rigid as he breathed on her ear in the manner of a man looking out the window at the sprawling expanse of mountainous terrain below.

"That is not a Heinkel bomber," he said, as surprised as she was. "What is going on?"

She turned, close enough to a kiss, and Didier moved back, sitting next to her without contact.

"What aircraft is that?" Konrad asked, seated a row back and not part of the firing line between Didier and the woman.

But the man was a follower. A scientist, but not a leader by any means.

"I think it is a Japanese design," Bertrand—Bertrand?!?—spoke up. "It appears similar to the Mitsubishi torpedo bomber they have started building."

Didier turned to the assassin and remembered to close his mouth from where it had fallen open as the man grinned.

American baseball, American radio crime dramas, and Japanese military aircraft?

Bertrand had the most complicated and unlikely set of interests, it seemed.

"What the hell is it doing up here?" Reiher demanded, a moment before Didier could do the same, so he supposed that he was required to have an opinion.

An answer.

However nice it was to see the woman at a loss for words, he was hardly better.

"Perhaps we are not the only players involved, then?" Didier asked. "We know they made it to Lahore, but should have left by now, according to your spies. What other spies might have stumbled across their path and seek to uncover Shirazi's secrets?"

He left it at that. Of all the people he had encountered on this quest, however tangentially, the Japanese had had no presence that he could remember.

Were they here for an entirely unrelated reason?

Had they already killed Shirazi and stolen a march, since this was the location the German spies had suggested the woman was headed for?

Too much unknown.

"We must go down and investigate," Didier announced when the others had fallen silent. "And we cannot simply destroy the craft from the air, as pleasant as that would be, because something is wrong. Tell the pilots to land, but not too closely, as whoever is down there might open fire, recognizing us as competition."

He focused on Konrad first, bending that man to his will. He would need Konrad when he was done with *Fraulein* Reiher.

Konrad rose with a heavy nod and made his way forward, leaving the woman alone with Didier.

And Bertrand.

"What do you suspect?" she asked, leaning closer, but in a conspiracy, instead of an assignation.

"Shirazi told someone that there was something here to find," Didier replied. "They came. We need to find out who and what, careful that the woman is not somehow behind us and sneaking up, as she had done to me before."

"Do we land, then send the aircraft off?"

"They lack the fuel for such a thing, unless they return directly to Kabul," Didier said. "Bertrand, what is the range of the Japanese plane?"

After all, if he had an expert at hand…

"Depending on load and model, at least four thousand kilometers," the assassin answered. "And a much higher ceiling than this Heinkel."

Didier nodded. The Imperial Japanese Navy was preparing for a war to the death with Britain and the Americans, practicing in China much as the Germans were in Spain.

"Then we must land and see what we can discover," Didier said. "We can always disable or destroy the craft. Or perhaps even steal it, as it sounds like a better craft than the one we have currently, no?"

He liked the way the woman bristled at the thought that perhaps the Aryan supermen weren't the most advanced and dangerous people in the world, but she didn't get outside of Europe much. The Americans, slow to anger, were terrible when roused. The Japanese, as well.

Konrad returned a moment later, nodding as he moved to Didier's former seat.

"We land shortly," he said. "They intend to fly low twice, seeing if anyone responds while determining the best place to set down."

The game had just gotten more complicated.

Most likely a trap.

Whose?

CHAPTER TWENTY-TWO

Zareen walked in the middle of the group, trailing both Ghada and Finn, while Emad brought up the rear behind Asher.

Already, she had done the impossible and proven all those fuddy-duddy old fools wrong, when they loudly proclaimed that it was impossible to travel fast enough to visit another star system.

Merely impossible with their current science, which, like aircraft she had recently learned, was leaping forward almost every year.

The hallway was comfortable and lit. Cool, but not as cold as the outside air.

They had considered closing the door, but decided that it was better to let outside air continue to circulate, in case the interior had been sealed up for...however long.

She pulled off a glove and touched the wall, mostly to try to understand it. Ghada had suggested that everything felt artificial, like concrete somehow poured into this shape to harden, hiding conduits and such while giving the impression of stone. She could not argue with that, just as she couldn't determine how the lights worked.

And they did. The first time a strip had gone out behind

them, Emad had barked a warning, but apparently they responded to motion, with some in the distance coming on as Ghada walked and those behind them slowly fading out.

By now, they had moved around several curves in the stone such that daylight no longer followed them. Zareen supposed that humans would have gone straight, but Asher has assured her that Durren liked things to flow naturally.

Then they came to a dead end. Of sorts. This hallway ended, and a staircase went up to the right. Carved into the stone in the same way that the others had. Perhaps by the same tools.

"Let us take a break here," Asher offered. "The air is dry and you need to drink water."

She agreed and took a few sips from her canteen, marveling at what they'd found. The air was also warmer than she'd been expecting, to the point that everyone had undone their jackets to let heat out, instead of trying to keep it in.

"Huh," Finn offered, squatting down and studying the staircase. "No dust at all. Asher, how did they do that?"

It was intriguing, watching the Man With No Face pause as if deep in thought.

"Our spacecraft had a life support system with air filters, Finn," Asher finally replied. "Dust would be pulled out of the air with an electrical charge, and then the metal surfaces would occasionally be cleaned. Possibly they have done something similar here, though as I remind you, I am a sociologist, not an engineer."

"Memories of how they did it are good enough," Finn nodded, rising. "Suggests that some of their systems might still be working."

Zareen agreed, but the lights were on, so something was.

Did it require Durren to maintain, or was it automated enough?

Or did they have other robots present, like Asher, capable of toiling away for years or centuries without complaint?

And what would they program their robots to do if confronted with humans inside their base like an infection?

Zareen squared her shoulders and nodded to Ghada to continue.

Up, into the heart of this mystery.

Whatever it was.

CHAPTER TWENTY-THREE

Didier had to admit that the Germans were prepared for the climate. Fur-lined flight suits like the pilots wore had been found for him and Bertrand. The color was almost enough to turn his stomach, but he would only be in Nazi gray for a short time.

The next French Republic would find their own fashion designer. One with a wider color template.

And better style.

But he didn't say that. Merely smiled as he closed the jumpsuit about halfway and joined Konrad and the *Fraulein* outside.

There had been no response from the Japanese plane, even when viewed from a slight distance though binoculars.

It appeared abandoned.

Didier still fell in behind the *Fraulein* and Bertrand as they walked.

Let them get shot first.

He didn't know if the .25 automatic in his pocket could bring down an aircraft, but it would penetrate most armors at short range. Rockets were like that.

Nothing. And nobody.

Bertrand squatted and ran his fingers through the dirt, studying things.

Then he moved back and forth, eyes still on the ground.

"Six people, I think," Bertrand said finally. "Four males and two females, at least by shoe size. One male moved around much more than the others."

He pointed and Didier nodded. He wasn't any sort of wilderness scout. That was why he had an assassin.

"Where did they go?" Reiher asked.

Bertrand moved around the aircraft, pointing to what looked to be one of the main canyons below the glacier.

"That way," he said simply. "Maybe as recently as yesterday, but I'm not familiar with this climate and terrain to be certain. Some of the tracks appear younger."

Didier pursed his lips and studied the sun.

They had flown overnight to get here early in the day, only an hour or so after dawn, needing sunlight to be sure what they saw.

Had the Japanese gotten here yesterday?

"Bertrand, check the aircraft," he ordered. "Are they really Japanese?"

"You suspect something?" Reiher asked as the two Germans moved close.

"They had an old Ford Trimotor at one point," Didier reminded them. "Then a stolen Heinkel. Perhaps they have found a new aircraft. The controls should all be in Japanese, in that case, unless someone has taken the time to redo everything in some other language."

She nodded.

Didier was playing a hunch, but couldn't have told even himself what it was.

Bertrand returned a moment later.

"Everything is written in ideograms," the assassin confirmed. "There are some boxes in the rear, but I didn't dig into them. Should I?"

"No," Didier decided. "Whoever it is has stolen a march on us and we need to catch up to them, wherein we can determine for ourselves."

He turned his gaze on the Germans like the Sphinx.

Fraulein Reiher nodded.

"We will leave the pilots here to guard both aircraft," she ordered Konrad. "And pack ourselves after whoever this is."

Didier nodded. They had some supplies, and could always destroy the Japanese craft later, then return to Kabul or wherever to get more.

But this mystery needed to be solved quickly.

Someone had definitely stolen a march on him, and Didier didn't like it one damned bit.

CHAPTER TWENTY-FOUR

Finn hadn't ever done something like this.

Oh, sure, guns and trouble. Almost his middle name.

Or what folks back home might have known him by, if anyone ever matched fingerprints.

Best not go there.

But underground spelunking. Or whatever this was.

Ghada moved like a ghost.

And he couldn't spend much time admiring her bottom. Not as dangerous as all this might turn out to be.

So he watched above her. Around her. Clearing the corners and relying on Asher to give a warning if he heard anything.

Because most folks didn't understand how good that fella's ears were.

Old stone. Clean, though, when he'd been expecting dust and stuff.

Like you got in an old house that had been closed up and abandoned for too long.

Except that the lights in here worked and they hadn't had to dig out their Coleman lantern or their flashlights. And Asher's suggestion of a heating and cooling system that was filtering things made sense, assuming it could be kept running smoothly.

That suggested hands. Robot hands, like Asher's, doing things to keep things running. Maintenance, like *Cerberus* and the California Condor had required on a regular basis, because things got old. Broke down. Wore out.

Human things.

What about Durren things?

They hit the top of the stairs and it was another hallway.

Except...

"Ghada, hang tight a second," he muttered just loud enough for her to hear.

She froze, knife in one hand like a Comanche raider ready to steal your horse.

Or your soul.

"What?" Ghada murmured back, head not turning.

Finn moved up next to her, then a little past where she could see him. Hans and Emad were all set to go Joshua at Jericho behind him, so Finn wasn't too worried.

He touched the left hand wall. Non-gun-side, because he had his Colt down by his side with the hammer back and the safety set.

Just like the rum running days.

"Walls are square," he said, pointing up and down to where this wasn't a tube, but a rectangle punched out of the mountain.

Floors still smooth. Lights like before.

Doors up ahead. Closed.

Would they open?

Who might be home?

"What does it mean?" Zareen asked.

Finn considered all sorts of weird scenarios. Helped that he'd occasionally been bored enough to pick up some of that pulp crap Hans read and meander through it.

Weird science usually more magic than anything, but Finn also remembered his first flight in a hunk of balsa and wire, covered over with canvas. Nothing at all like *Sunrise*, out on that lake bed.

And no way in hell he could have predicted that, twenty years ago.

"Asher," Finn said. "If the Durren liked things smooth and curvy, did someone else maybe build this part? Maybe earlier, and maybe the Durren did the staircase down and the corridor to the surface?"

Had that feel. Older yet, though he had no clue about the aliens and how long they'd been doing things.

Except that Asher knew a lot of old languages and the only way to do that was to come down here and talk to folks.

Asher walked to the seam where the square bits gave way to the stairwell. Ran fingers up it like a human would, but Finn didn't know how much of that was an affectation, and how much he was like them.

Just like Finn would have done it.

"I believe that you may be correct, Finn," Asher said after a moment. "The stone was cut with different technology. I will not try to explain beyond that, as it would do no good. But yes, I think someone older than the Durren did this."

Finn nodded and watched forward again. That had niggled at the back of his head. Now he understood why.

"How old is Durren civilization?" Zareen asked.

"Extremely old, Zareen," Asher answered. "However, I have hints that there are others out there, though little of that was added to my programming. The map makes sense, if perhaps the Durren took over a base made earlier by someone else, in turn adapting it to their needs. China and the Near East have both been centers of advanced civilization for a long time, and a location such as this is somewhat central to both."

Finn nodded. Iron age supposedly started around the time of Homer and the Trojan War, so maybe three thousand years ago, give or take. Bronze before that, and some of those pyramids he used to fly over regular-like were a bunch older, if the stories were even halfway true.

Folks watching this place for a long time, trying to decide how crazy humans really were?

Lots of crazy. Any historian could tell you that.

"Do we expect anyone or anything in one of those rooms?" Ghada asked.

She hadn't stopped watching forward.

"I would doubt it," Asher replied.

"What about folks like you?" Finn interjected. "Robots and such?"

"It is possible, Finn," Asher confirmed. "However, if they are programmed to harm humans, there is little at all any of you might do to stop them. If they have not been, then they may simply ignore all of you."

"What about you, Asher?" Zareen asked.

"They may recognize me as one of them," he said. "And I shall attempt to communicate with them at that time, but I hardly know more than any of you. And, I will remind you, my existence is a criminal act by a splinter group of Durren scientists, so any robots or organics we encounter may prove more hostile to me than you. Keep that in mind."

"Will do," Finn said, nodding to Ghada to start her stalk again.

Thing were about to get interesting.

CHAPTER TWENTY-FIVE

Ghada moved forward to the first door. It was open, but unlit and she stopped outside to look in, wondering at some of the shapes she saw.

A shelf that might be a bed, from the length, but it stuck out of the wall without resting on anything. And appeared to be some sort of orangish stone, rather than metal, contrasting against the more gray stone.

Stepping to the door, she automatically reached for a light switch before she caught herself.

Lights came on anyway, but when she looked, Ghada saw no switch. Merely a round light about the size of her palm, currently a soft blue.

Intrigued, she waved her hand at it a second time and it turned green.

And the overhead light went out.

"Huh," she muttered, turning it on and stepping deeper to allow Finn entrance.

Except that Zareen stepped in, leaving the men in the hallway.

"This controls the lights," Ghada demonstrated, then turned back.

"Dresser?" Zareen mused.

Ghada looked. Inset in the wall, but slightly out, as though drawers, so at least something she understood visually. She approached and noted a pair of handles, such as she might have done them. Rings, in a silvery metal without tarnish.

She tugged and the top came open smoothly, revealing emptiness inside. She went to pull it the rest of the way, but something held it, so Ghada squatted down instead to look under it. Rails of some sort. Still working. Nothing hidden underneath, as Asher had described the money he had stolen from Beauchêne in Cairo.

A hand to the back to check there as well revealed nothing. Quickly, Ghada did the others.

Nothing.

Still, something new. Something alien, even. Hopefully, she would be able to find some token that had been overlooked.

Assuming the place really was abandoned.

She turned to Zareen with a question in her eyes.

"We can be more thorough later," Zareen decided. "For now, let us see how deeply we can penetrate this ancient edifice. And what secrets it might reveal when we do."

Ghada nodded and returned to the hallway, taking her spot at the head of the column as she began to work her way inward, past more of what she wanted to call individual hotel rooms.

Somewhere, there would be shops. Storage, hopefully not emptied out.

And maybe, just maybe, people.

CHAPTER TWENTY-SIX

Asher listened, on a much wider range of frequencies than humans were capable of.

Faintly, as if in a great distance, the hum of machines that took him back to the craft that had intended to deliver him to Earth. And had, but badly.

Still, that metallic hum of fans and systems.

He presumed another atomic pile such as the small one that powered him, but on a much larger scale. Thorium, because it was a useful element that didn't translate itself well to weaponry.

He had read the musings of Einstein and others on such things as could possibly be done with Uranium and Plutonium.

Thus, the Durren probably expected humanity to destroy itself with atomic weaponry before becoming a space-borne threat to galactic civilization.

And they might be right, in spite of anything Asher might do to dissuade or deflect them first.

Humans.

Little other sound. Not even drips of water, suggesting to him that the facility had been properly sealed in its time and either maintained or that well designed.

Except that they had built it close to the point where the Indian plate and the Asian plate were tectonically interacting. Groundquakes would be constant. Big ones would occur frequently enough that the base faced the challenge of entropy.

All of which added up to an expectation of other robots. Perhaps automated and autonomous systems left behind by departing Durren to keep the facility in readiness.

He cataloged a new emotion, but wasn't entirely sure what to call it. Anticipation, tinged with worry, because he might be about to meet his own kind? And they might be hostile, because he had been delivered to this world as an A.S.H.E.R., Mark Seven, and had remade himself into the Mark Eight—possibly Nine by now—version without their help.

Or hindrance.

Or, as Finn might have described it, adult supervision.

Still, dread.

No footsteps approached, but autonomous units might be programmed to walk quietly. He had not, but he had been a social unit, intended to meet and interact with humans, rather than being largely invisible and ignorable.

"More stairs ahead," Ghada said loud enough for everyone else to hear. "Different, this time. More square. Deeper tread. Shorter rise."

Asher studied them from this distance and knew them to predate the Durren.

How odd, that he could learn such things from his human friends to decipher elements of civilization from the remains they left behind.

Was he also becoming something of an archaeologist as well? His original programming had been limited to human interaction, but chance had delivered him to Egypt, at a period in Human history when the British and others had begun a more thorough study of the Pharonic period of Egyptian history, learning and understanding those men and women who had originally lifted up the pyramids thousands of years ago.

What else might he learn about those beings who had been here before the Durren?

And who were they? His programming had not included much of anything about life beyond Earth's atmosphere.

Asher found himself cross with the fools who had so limited him, when he might have been able to create more robust and detailed matrices of behavioral comparison.

A blink and Asher understood that a human would have a cold spot in his or her belly.

Fear signal.

The Durren didn't need the matrix. They were either going to conquer the humans, or tip them back into the barbarism they had emerged from some ten thousand years ago.

Another chance to grow up better, before they became advanced and more dangerous.

He would have growled. All of the signs lined up and agreed on that point.

The Durren were enemies of humanity, not potential saviors.

The others were keeping humans ignorant for their own safety. The Durren were planning to intervene.

One way or the other.

He would have something to say about that.

CHAPTER TWENTY-SEVEN

Didier disliked physical activity.

Sweat was for peasants, not scholars and scientists. There was a reason he employed Bertrand, and not just because the man liked to kill people.

Still, it was necessary, for as long as the *Fraulein* continued to plague his existence.

He could see that change coming sooner and sooner, with each heavy step he took up the canyon.

"Hsst!" Reiher whistled.

Didier looked up from where he'd been walking and noted a dark spot in the distance.

Bertrand motioned him off to one side, so he and Konrad took as much shelter as they could behind a few scraggly bushes and some rocks, pitiful little though it was.

The two killers joined them a moment later.

"A campsite," Reiher said quietly. "Someone has set up a tent, but I did not see anyone about. No sign of a fire."

Of course not. There is nothing here to burn.

He smiled indulgently at the woman.

"Bertrand, you stalk the camp and see if anyone is around," Didier ordered.

"And me?" the *Fraulein* asked arrogantly.

"Join him, if you wish," Didier indulged. "Konrad and I will remain here and watch."

Damned if you do, damned if you don't?

Didier smiled at her eyeblink of a snarl, then the woman turned and began walking in that direction.

Didier waited until those two were out of earshot, then turned to Konrad.

"I hope the woman doesn't get herself killed," he murmured. "Has she always been so rambunctious?"

"Generally, yes," Konrad nodded. "She has had luck on her side. And ferocity."

Didier could testify to the latter, much to his dismay.

"Would the Nazi Party immediately claim any discoveries we make, or will they allow the scientists time to understand such things first?" he asked obliquely.

Konrad scowled at him, face pinched.

"They are the same thing, Beauchêne," Konrad said. "But I understand your question. The Party expects us to create newer and better weapons for them."

Didier nodded.

Anything he discovered would be stolen by the Germans almost immediately.

It would be critical timing then, for some terrible accident to befall the *Fraulein* first, and then Konrad after that, before the man was able to communicate to Berlin what he might have found.

And it would need to be done in such a way that the pilots they had left behind wouldn't suspect a double-cross. Triple-cross?

Didier would need at least one pilot, because neither he nor Bertrand could fly the aircraft.

Once he got to Kabul, however...

Or maybe some other place where the Germans would not

immediately think to look for him, much as Shirazi had gone to Lahore instead of Tunguska.

Yes, misdirection would be necessary. Perhaps more necessary in the future.

He turned to watch Bertrand and that damnable woman approach someone's camp, prepared for violence.

Nobody emerged.

Bertrand even stuck his head into the tent carefully, then turned and waved for Didier and Konrad to join them.

The hike started him sweating again, just as he had cooled enough to be comfortable.

He grumbled as he walked.

"The same footprints as at the aircraft," Bertrand confirmed. "I recognize two of the boot prints directly."

"Where are they?" Didier asked

The *Fraulein* pointed to more tracks, heading back and into a small defile on the right. Narrow and a shade steeper.

Lovely.

"Who are they?" Didier asked.

The two shrugged.

"Most of the gear is generic," Bertrand replied. "English, but if they were close enough to Shirazi to learn about this place, they might have also been in Lahore with her."

Didier grimaced.

Perhaps it was her and her gangsters. That made the most sense, having traded aircraft yet again to throw him off their trail.

"We follow," Didier announced, simply taking charge of things because he was tired of listening to the two Aryan fools dictate policy.

Or any of the other Aryan fools.

Maybe Germany would need to be subsumed into a Fourth French Republic, much as it had been under Napoleon.

Yes, that put a smile on his face.

Bertrand led. Didier followed the woman, with Konrad trailing for now.

Then they found the staircase carved into the stone itself.

"Yes," Didier replied to Bertrand's unasked question. "Up."

This was what Shirazi had been seeking, obviously. They had flown here, perhaps following some map or maybe the Man With No Face had divulged some of his secrets.

The tribesmen of the Tibetan plateau had not done this thing.

Who had?

He began to ascend, seeking his destiny.

CHAPTER TWENTY-EIGHT

Zareen studied the walls. The ceiling. The various tidbits that they saw. Part of it was simple and primitive, but the lights defied explanation.

And they had ascended another staircase, finding a level of larger rooms. Empty in ways that suggested stock rooms. Storage, with all the shelving removed, having left marks on the floor open to interpretation.

Whatever interpretation she wished to apply.

And that was all she could do at present.

Guess.

The lights worked. Air stirred when she paused to feel that faint breeze on her cheeks.

"Hey, that's interesting," Finn called from a corner of yet another of these large rooms that nobody could explain.

Zareen moved close. The others drifted in as well.

Finn was pointing at the ground.

"Lines," he said. "Etched into the floor. Square. Almost feels like..."

"What?" she practically demanded.

"A lift," he said. "Cargo elevator kind of thing."

He leaned back and they both studied the ceiling, some

fifteen feet overhead. The lines in the floor seemed to line up with matching ones above.

"I wanna try something," he said, walking to the wall nearby, where the usual light switch seemed to reside, save that this one was red at present. "Everybody on, but ready to hop off if I'm wrong."

The group joined, each near an edge.

Finn touched the red light and the roof retracted with a bit of a grind, revealing sudden lights from another level above them. At the same time, the floor began to rise, exactly where he had apparently expected.

So, cargo elevator, which suggested that the area above them was a loading dock.

Which suggested a place where alien spacecraft landed to disgorge cargo.

Zareen found that she was holding her breath as they ascended, and forced herself to breathe normally and slowly.

Cathedral, as if built by giants, with stone vaulted at least two hundred feet overhead.

As they emerged, the space was larger than a football pitch. Maybe three of them, side by side for a tournament. Perfectly flat in ways that felt unnatural.

More lights coming on overhead, though she could see more than one place where half a fixture had seemingly failed. Or sections weren't working.

Zareen wasn't sure if the fact that aliens could fail filled her with joy or dismay. They had crashed when bringing Asher. But still built this place in some distant past.

A bollard rose when they did, with a similar red button, right where Finn could touch it again to presumably lower things back down, transferring cargo for storage.

"Physics is physics," she said, drawing all eyes. "Loading dock. Cargo elevator. Store rooms. Cabins for crew and staff. Remarkably similar to humans."

"The Durren are, in many ways," Asher replied. "At least

physically. Culturally and emotionally, the differences outweigh the similarities, generally."

She nodded. He had told her as much as he could remember, seemingly. And would learn more here than she would, because he could read things she could only guess at.

"This way," Finn announced, starting to walk towards a nearby wall.

Zareen started to ask why, when she saw a doorway, next to a wide picture window that would be the perfect place to sit and supervise ships coming and going.

If humans were involved.

This was alien, wasn't it?

Or were humans some strange descendant of aliens, like angels fallen? Garden of Eden as another planet, with Adam and Eve exiled to Earth?

Or Noah carrying his family and friends from some ancient conflagration or catastrophe on another world?

Zareen had never given much credence to the Christian bible, save as a source of strange and interesting stories that were supposedly representative of older things.

How old?

How strange?

How much was there to learn?

She followed Finn into the office and watched him turn on the lights.

CHAPTER TWENTY-NINE

Didier noted the open door on the fourth landing, gasping from the climb out of the various valleys below him.

And sweating like a peasant almost enough to cast this stupid suit from him and burn it in disgust.

Bertrand had already moved to the door and looked in.

"Corridor into and under the mountain," he said quickly. "Do we follow?"

"I cannot see how we do not," Didier replied acidly.

Someone had not only stolen a march on him, but seemingly had gotten almost to whatever treasure might await at the center, like ancient fables of dragons with hoards of gold.

Perhaps it would eat Shirazi for him and make Didier's life easier.

Assuming he could somehow slay a dragon after that.

He was no St. George. Except for the .25 automatic in his pocket that might qualify as a lance.

Didier moved to the door. Studied the mechanism that held it, as much as he could. Which wasn't much.

Metal. Not an alloy he recognized at first touch. Light and strong. Set on a continuous pin hinge such that it might work for centuries.

Which was exactly his fear.

How many centuries?

He pulled out a flashlight Konrad had given him and shined it into the hole. Dark, straight, dry.

Not a sewer, then, but a corridor.

And whoever was ahead of him had seemingly come this way, leaving it open behind them.

Because they didn't know they were being followed?

Or did?

Didier growled and took a step inside, amazed when lights came on.

He paused and felt a breeze blowing into his face when he looked outside again, suggesting some sort of chimney effect drawing fresh air into the mountain.

And suggesting how big the place might be, if it did so.

He undid as much of the flight suit as he could without taking it off, then went ahead and stripped back down to his suit and tie.

French fashion, instead of German.

If I am going to be eaten by a dragon, I don't want your gods mistaking me for one of you, Fraulein.

He smiled and gestured for Bertrand to do the same, casting his suit to a spot where the door closing might be interrupted.

But honestly, he was tired of the damned thing and willing to risk a chill.

Konrad and Reiher remained suited up, but unbuttoned them against heat.

As you wish.

Didier studied the depths visible. Came to his decision.

"Forward, Bertrand," he ordered, suddenly tired of this entire charade. "Someone is ahead of us and we must locate them."

He glared at the two Nazi fools enough to draw them into his wake and followed his assassin into the depths.

CHAPTER THIRTY

Emad paused to wonder at how far he had come on this quest, from the depths of the Cyrenaican desert to the top of the world, following Zareen and her dream.

And her as a woman, but that was always going to come second.

Ridding his homeland of those Italian ticks was a glorious first step to freeing Egypt and Persia. Making over the whole world without the domination of the Europeans.

A man could dream.

Today, he found himself almost utterly lost, surrounded by architecture and designs that he had no grounding to understand.

His confusion must have shown, because Hans stepped close.

"Shipping office, if we were there," he announced. "Clerks here and here, though from the height of the counter I presume that they stand, like at a bank, rather than sit. That window behind us keeps noise and wind out when the door is closed. More offices back that way where Finn and Zareen are exploring."

Emad nodded, grateful.

"Was this some sort of commercial port, then?" he asked.

"Airport, perhaps," Hans nodded. "Craft coming and going, but maybe as many hauling people as cargo, with scientists come to see the primitives. Still need to feed people, and I have no idea…Hey, Asher, what do Durren eat?"

Emad turned as Asher perked up, then slumped slightly, as if in confusion.

"It is hard to say, my friend," Asher said, stepping close. "There was a device in the wall with digital controls. Someone would walk up and speak to it, or select a number more likely. A bit later, it would beep and you could open the door to reveal food or drink."

"Huh," Hans grunted. "An automat."

"You are familiar with such a thing?" Emad asked.

"Germany invented them," Hans beamed. "Quisisana opened in Berlin in 1895. I'm presuming this version was much more sophisticated, but that's a question of technology, rather than culture. The Durren sound remarkably similar to us."

"They are," Asher agreed. "Physically. As to the food and drink, I seem to recall that most of it was derived from vegetable stock, or proteins grown in large vats, rather than animals slaughtered. Drink consisted of things like tea or coffee, often with additional flavorings added in a manner similar to your various brands of soft drinks, and some level of carbonation was common."

"Fizzy drinks make the world go round," Hans assured both of them with a deep, scholarly nod, then he broke into a grin that made Emad feel better.

"Is there such a device around here?" Emad asked.

"I have not seen such a thing, but I also was not looking," Asher noted apologetically. "I shall look. If this is such as you have described it, I would expect a kitchen or break room to be located back through there."

Emad followed his finger.

"Finn," Emad called, causing the others to look up. "Asher

suggests a break room with equipment. Come, Asher, let us look."

He led, headed back down a corridor lined with doors that opened when a handle was turned. Remarkably similar to anything he knew, but Zareen and others had noted that basic physics did not change, and that the Durren would end up using tools that humans would find comfortable.

The rooms were too small for people to live, so Emad presumed offices where clerks might work, building on Hans's logic of a shipping office. Each was stripped to the walls, leaving marks in the floor where furniture had once rested, but nothing else remained.

A larger office at the back looked to be two smaller ones with the wall between them removed.

"Try this one," Asher suggested.

Emad opened the one at the end of the hall and found a much larger space. The entire width of hallway and both sides of the offices, twice as deep.

Again, bare. As always, a light switch that would immediately bring illumination.

Asher walked by him while Emad turned to take the room in, stopping in front of a wall.

Emad heard Asher speak something, but couldn't begin to understand it. Tonal, like some of the Asian languages from what he'd heard.

A light on the wall came on, and something answered.

Emad drew close and saw a spot on the wall light up, with what looked like a block of buttons, but nothing raised. Blue, with brighter lines outlining.

More conversation. Less understanding.

The others drew close.

Asher shrugged finally and turned to look at Emad.

"The machine was emptied at some point," he said. "Presumably when the rest of the facility was, but the machine does not have any more information than that."

"But it does work?" Emad clarified.

"It does," Asher nodded. "And could be reloaded, if someone brought more supplies. My expectation is that the facility is being maintained, but we have not seen anyone responsible, as yet."

"Robots, like you?" Hans asked.

"Yes," Asher agreed. "Presumably."

"Let's go find them," Hans said.

Emad found himself agreeing.

They were so close.

CHAPTER THIRTY-ONE

Hans was practically giddy with anticipation, but he also knew himself to be a nerd on the topic. Pulp magazines were a cheap, easy way to practice his English, and he had consumed everything he could lay his hands on, from early private detective stuff to the *scientifiction* that was prominent today.

Far too many stories of aliens and robots and travelers, and he was here, in the middle of an alien base, hidden in the Himalayan mountains like some ancient fable. With a robot companion.

Maybe those fables had been onto something?

Maybe they weren't fables?

The possibilities were endlessly fascinating, as he fell into step with Asher, the others strung out behind them.

Hans kept watch, but the rifle was slung across his back for now, and a pistol he had gotten from Magdy was easily at hand if he needed it, though he expected the others to all be faster and better shots.

He fixed things. Mostly aircraft. Flew occasionally. Had no war stories like Finn, doing things in the States during Prohibition that had been loud and violent.

No, Hans had seen Weimar rise, and start to fall from the

inside, before he'd left to find work in Italy, of all places. Not exactly the brightest idea, but it had gotten him eventually connected with Finn.

And the others.

And the grandest adventure of all!

He took care not to skip and hum as he followed one alien robot in search of others.

The machines worked. It had talked to Asher. Others might, as well.

Zareen would have her proof. And whatever trouble she intended to cause with it.

It would be good trouble. Righteous.

Earth-shaking.

Hans followed.

The bay was huge. Maybe not long enough for an aircraft to take off, but Hans presumed anti-gravity fields that let them ascend without lifting wings. Strange ray guns and things.

All sorts of fun.

Back out and across Asher led them.

The field was flat. Empty.

CLEAN, which didn't happen. Robot janitors?

Something.

Asher said he could survive at least a century, and that had been undercover and on his own, for a mission intended to only last a few years.

Battery packs you could recharge, if they were inside a base and never needed to leave? Hans had seen some early electric vehicles, when petroleum had been so expensive. The technology hadn't kept up, so you had internal combustion engines these day, but what could aliens teach humanity?

And how could he go home and throw those stupid Nazis out with the trash?

Bismark had given them a nice country, even if that idiot Wilhelm had fucked it all up with his dreams of adequacy and imperial glory. Better that the fool lived in exile in the Netherlands. Now they needed to get rid of Hitler as well. And the rest of them.

Hans caught himself short of growing angry and looking for ray guns he could take back to Germany. Mostly.

Asher was headed towards a different wall, squared off and artificial like the tunnels below had been from the way other parts had been left mostly raw.

A door. Closed. Locked, apparently, because the handle refused to open when Asher attempted it. And when he spoke, it didn't respond. Just that light where you could do things, but nothing.

Asher sighed and turned to face all of them.

"Someone with more paranoia left this part of the facility secured," Asher said. "There is a password, but it was not on the map. I have reviewed those notes."

Hans nodded. First smart thing the aliens had done yet, though he supposed that hiding the first door almost qualified, since they'd left a code to open it.

Or the Durren had.

Had they come along later and not been able to access all of the base they had found? Was that why they added that door and carved other tunnels?

How many alien civilizations were out there, anyway? Maybe as many as Earth? More?

Hans turned to Finn.

"Chicago?" he asked, a shorthand they had developed over three years of long flights in the middle of nowhere, with nothing to do but chat.

Finn grimaced, but Hans had been expecting that.

"Yeah, probably," Finn sighed. "Stand back."

Hans grabbed Asher by the arm and pulled him off to one side. The others moved away.

Finn took a deep breath and flexed his shoulders as Hans watched.

CHAPTER THIRTY-TWO

Finn didn't like to go back to his gangster days. Left all that behind when Prohibition ended, because the States had started looking better, but he was wanted in too many places.

Way easier making a living back in Europe.

But the big Kraut was right.

Chicago.

Technically, more of a Milwaukee thing, but he didn't correct the fellow.

Chicago was just angry at him.

Them folks in Milwaukee were likely still *pissed*.

Just because, he had the Colt in one hand, hammer back and safety locked where he could drop it and be firing before the rest of his brain caught up with trouble.

That had kept him alive more than once.

He concentrated on the door. Looked like a lot of them had. Handle. Flat face. Maybe aluminum when he'd heard Asher and Hans tap on it. Hollow, rather than solid, because otherwise that was a crapton of aluminum, just for a door.

How rich were Zareen's aliens?

Probably rich enough.

But Chicago was called for.

Finn moved a little to his left and a bit forward. Took a deep breath. Reared up like an angry mule and kicked right next to the handle about as hard as he could.

Something bent.

He kicked it a second time. More movement, but he was blowing pretty hard.

"Finn, allow me," Asher said, gesturing.

Finn staggered a step back to where Ghada caught him.

Asher nodded and punched the door, right in the same spot Finn had been kicking.

Something broke this time. Metal tearing sound.

Door flew inwards until it hit a stop with a bong like a church bell.

"Chicago?" Asher asked curiously.

"Gangsters occasionally had to kick in a door to get the drop on someone inside," Finn said. "Kept them from having time to draw a gun or open fire through the door. Most of the doors I've ever known were wood, though. Same with the frames, so you can kick them in. This one was a bit tougher."

Asher nodded and pointed.

"Be careful not to touch this part, as the shearing metal would have heated to a level that it would leave burns for the next several minutes."

Finn nodded at that. Asher was a lot stronger than he looked.

Just didn't have a criminal mind that let him understand how to do certain things.

Good thing he had friends.

Finn led, because he was closest.

Colt in one hand, he reached across and brought the lights up.

Big room. Felt like a lobby in a hotel or a corporate office, intending to impress you with scale.

And pretty.

Designs in the walls that looked like different metals, rather than paint. Golds, silvers, bronzes, but he didn't know what they actually were. Asher might.

No furniture, but that was nothing new. If they'd emptied the soda machine, they were serious about those sorts of things.

Lights. Ceiling up where a second floor could have hung, making things pretty and bright in here.

"Asher, what is this place?" Zareen asked, standing right next to him when Finn glanced over.

"A control facility," Asher replied. "City hall, for the base, perhaps? I am not sure how to describe it, save that what you ultimately seek should be here somewhere, though I have doubts, given the completeness with which this place was previously stripped."

"Who stripped it?" Finn asked.

"I presume the Durren," Asher nodded. "And I agree with you that it appears to be older, so perhaps they were tomb robbers in the manner of the English gentlemen who have so assiduously stocked the British Museum, despite the wishes of the local governments involved. This place feels looted."

Finn caught Zareen's bristle, but that was her British side. And he knew the Scots weren't always as keen on such things, having been on the short end of the English so many times. And officially for the last couple of centuries.

The British were stuffy and obnoxious, but usually believed that they were saving art from barbarians. It was the barbarians that complained.

Part of the reason his folks had kicked the Brits out after 1776.

Maybe it was Egypt's turn.

Then Persia.

Finn nodded and took a long stride inwards. There were doors he could see. Places where things had been sitting on the marble stone underfoot then removed or stripped.

Maybe the Durren had looted it.

Wasn't that kinda what he and Zareen were here for? Maybe they'd get lucky yet.

CHAPTER THIRTY-THREE

Didier felt so much better without that damned wool-lined jumpsuit. Almost human again.

No more peasant sweat, though both Konrad and the *Fraulein* were beginning to develop a musk.

Aryan supermen, indeed.

Bertrand had taken them inwards. Lights that came up and then turned off after a period, either in reaction to motion or sound. Empty rooms he took to be cabins, such as on an airship or marine vessel, as they were stylized in a similar manner.

Nothing whatsoever to indicate who had built this place, save that Didier could not think of a single mechanism wherein he could even explain the lights overhead, let alone replicate them.

He kept his misgivings to himself, though.

This original quest had been to prove that aliens had visited Earth. And done so more than once. And left behind traces that might be turned into inventions he could use to conquer the rest of the world.

If his *Aryan Übermenschen* associates didn't already know that, Didier saw no reason to educate and enlighten them on the topic.

They came to a thing that Didier could only classify as an art installation, as it made no sense mechanically.

"It's a lift," Bertrand announced, after a minute looking at it. "In the up position. We're looking at the piston, like a car up where a mechanic can get to the underside."

Suddenly, everything rotated in place and Didier saw it. He walked to a spot with a light and noted that it felt like a control switch.

"Everyone out of the way," he warned the Germans. Bertrand was already moving away.

Didier touched the light and the platform retracted, lowering and settling next to him on silent hydraulics that were all the more impressive when he noted the thickness of the plate itself. Even some light alloy would still be moving a great deal of mass.

"Do we suppose they went this way ahead of us?" the *Fraulein* asked, drawing her damnable Luger and holding it with a smile he could only classify as *hungry*.

"Presumably," Didier agreed. Then went ahead and pulled out his .25 automatic.

Better safe than sorry, as the old saying went.

He stepped onto the platform and waited for the others to join him. Bertrand had taken to carrying a Colt 1911 .45 Officer's Model similar to the one that the American gangster Severijns had shot him with, so Didier expected some foolish showdown at high noon, the man having listened to too many cowboy radio dramas on top of everything else.

Didier drew a breath and hoped that Shirazi and her posse weren't immediately waiting for them a level above, having seen the platform move.

Or whoever had gotten here ahead of him.

It didn't matter. He and Bertrand were the only two making it out alive later. The German pilots would have to be convinced that some alien device had proven inimical. Lethal.

Something.

He was done sharing his discoveries.

Didier triggered the control, and began to ascend into the realms of the gods on alien technology.

CHAPTER THIRTY-FOUR

Zareen allowed Finn to lead in his stance as protector. He and the others were like that, while not expecting that she needed anything except protection.

And it let her think, with less concern about her surroundings. Asher had suggested that the Durren had stripped the place in the distant past. Like English adventurers intent on looting ancient graves.

This felt like a palace that had been sacked so thoroughly that she couldn't even identify rooms, let along purposes. Surely, some were offices, while others were for sleeping, but the empty walls refused to divulge their secrets to her.

"Asher, are there any signs anywhere, indicating things?" she finally asked, catching up to the man who was studying it as they went down yet another hallway.

"I can see traces of wear in the floor, Zareen," he said, looking down. "There are spots next to each door, similar to the Automat we found below, but they have been deactivated or at least locked sufficiently to keep me from accessing them. Presumably, someone who was supposed to be here could have opened the door we forced, and thus brought everything back to active readiness."

"And we cheated," she nodded.

Asher shrugged.

"Humans are an unknown quantity to the Durren," he said. "At the same time, they maintained a low opinion, so I would expect them to take actions to prevent barbarians from accessing the facility. Certainly, even modern weapons would have been hard pressed to force the outer door by which we gained entrance into the mountain. Explosives could have destroyed the inner door, but if you cannot turn the machines on, most of this is merely a shell."

Perhaps a shell. She could already see bringing in a few mechanics to dismantle certain devices, in order to see how they worked.

And perhaps tools hard enough to cut off chunks of some of those alloys, that she might find a way to recreate them at a grander scale. Better armor for machines and people. More robust metals for better machines.

Whatever it would take to complete her own mission. While maintaining secrecy.

Zareen considered her mission halfway successful.

Now she needed to complete the second half and call it good.

They came to double doors that capped the current hallway. Finn and Asher stood before them like art critics, deep in thought with occasional murmurs.

She stepped close.

"What do we expect to find behind this?" she asked.

"Backstage," Finn replied before Asher could. "Everything up until now is the public-facing stuff. This feels like the part where you are in the loading docks, storage, and back offices that only employees get to see. Less pretty stuff."

"Less pretty?" she inquired.

"He suggests that this might be the location where our theoretical maintenance and repair robots would be located, Zareen," Asher interjected. "A nest, if you will, though the term does not translate well out of Durren into any language you speak."

She bristled for a moment, then considered that Asher knew the breadth of her linguistic capabilities. Persian. Arabic. English. Scottish. French. German. Italian. And a variety of dialects of each, some mutually incomprehensible, even a few villages apart.

And none of them could encompass what Asher expected to see behind this barrier?

Still, adventuress.

"Can you open it?" she said.

"Easy as pie," Finn said. "Been considering the implications. Y'all be ready to run like hell if something goes wrong when I do."

He had eyes fixed on her, and Zareen scowled. Then considered that she might yet be the slowest person here, if only because the others were all physically active people.

Still, she nodded.

This door might be the culmination of her entire quest.

Finn nodded back. Moved to that light that opened doors. Pressed it and moved back to the center as the double doors folded away inwards.

Zareen gasped.

CHAPTER THIRTY-FIVE

Well, crap. Finn had seen a lot of things in his time, from the farms of Montana to the trenches and skies of France to most of North Africa.

None of it had prepared him. Nor had Asher, but the fellow had tried.

Racks, three levels high. More'n half of them filled with shiny robots about the color of a good champagne, that rose gold you got.

Asher was a dull silver like brushed nickel underneath those robes. And built different. Knobs for joints. Tubes for limbs. Ball for a head. All of it originally intended to disappear beneath a fake hide that would make him look human.

These almost looked like skinny guys with armor suits on, except that they were solid. Thighs like his as he stepped into the room. Knees that were a turned-sideways cylinder. Blunt fingers like gauntlets.

Like nobody had ever intended them to appear as anything but what they were.

He remembered seeing the silent movie Metropolis back about a decade ago in a theater in Chicago. These folks looked like cousins of the robot in the film. And that had been a skinny woman inside.

He was a dozen steps in now, drawn by the beauty of it all.

Three levels. Hundreds of such machines, but none of them awake right now.

Hopefully.

He found he was okay with that idea. Better them off and waiting than awake and complaining about burglars.

Not like his intentions in here were all that good, after all.

Darker lights overhead. Dim, like some of the movies he'd seen where they wanted you thinking scary thoughts. Not dark. Just not as bright.

Like these machines didn't need it. And if they were off, they didn't. Asher had said he could see almost as well in the dark as he could in the light, so maybe the lighting was for the people.

Assuming he qualified.

"Zareen?" he called loud enough.

She came up on one side. Asher on the other. The rest spread out close, but it was an awe-inspiring moment.

Finn wouldn't have said he didn't believe, but he might not have ever expected something like this, that was for sure.

"Now what the hell do we do?" he asked.

Her mission. Asher's knowledge.

He just flew. And occasionally shot people.

"Asher?" she asked. "Are they working?"

"They are in a form of sleep, Zareen," he said. "There is a central intelligence that will direct them, however autonomous each instance might be."

"Queen bee?" Hans asked.

"As good a description as any, yes," Asher agreed. "Through there, I think."

"They likely to wake up while we're here?" Finn asked.

"I do not think so, Finn," Asher replied. "Assuming that the central control unit has not awakened to our presence, which it does not appear to have done."

"Or it's a trapdoor spider, waiting for us to get in too deep to escape," Finn suggested.

Didn't like to think those thoughts, but someone had to.

"That is also possible," Asher agreed. "Come, let us see what awaits."

Finn nodded and fell in beside the fellow.

Kinda like coming home for him, if the Man With No Face could be said to have one outside the slums and souqs of Cairo.

Still, they were about to find out.

CHAPTER THIRTY-SIX

Didier gazed at the space with barely concealed wonder at war with barely concealed terror.

Enormous. Gargantuan.

He wasn't sure any language contained the terms he wished to use to describe this space.

An alien cathedral, left entirely empty.

"Beauchêne."

Konrad drew his attention to a nearby door, open with a light on. Didier nodded Bertrand in motion that way, following a few steps behind.

This, Didier felt as if he could explain. It almost took him back to that warehouse on the edge of Cairo, where he had first captured Zareen Shirazi and her friends for interrogation, before the American gangster and the others had interrupted them. And shot out a tire in their escape.

Office. Low walled counter dividing the two sides, with space behind that where desks would have been, and a hallway that went back.

The lights were on in here. Most of the places they had seen were dark, save for where Bertrand had discovered how to bring the overhead lights up.

Someone had done the same here. Whoever it was that had flown up to this plateau in a Japanese aircraft. Had broken into the side of the mountain. Had found everything first.

Didier would have words for them, but he would at least thank whoever it had been for opening the way for him first.

Then he would kill them to preserve his secrets.

And either learn to fly, or hire Bertrand a minion or girlfriend who was a pilot, so that they could steal such aircraft later. Didier had a vision of the perfect French woman, and she was not in the mold of Shirazi, except perhaps shape. And local hill tribe barbarian women were not on his list.

But aircraft had suddenly become an important factor in his life, and he needed to be more mobile.

After the Germans were done.

"Back?" Bertrand asked in a whisper.

Didier nodded. It felt like they were close behind their prey now, so the assassin was moving like a hunter. No doubt, at least one knife was close at hand, but he retained the enormous Colt.

Gunfight at the OK Corral, or whatever silliness the Americans called it.

Hallway. Offices. Break room?

It had that larger space feel, but was too clean to be merely a storage room. Lights on one wall intrigued him, so Didier moved over. Instead of a simple switch, this appeared to be a series of buttons in rows and columns. Backlit, but he could not feel anything. The wall simply glowed, in the same manner that the lights overhead did.

Still, whatever machine was there responded when he pressed, because icons appeared above it. Changed as he pushed other buttons.

"What is it?" the *Fraulein* asked in a quiet, reverent voice.

"An alien machine," Didier replied, bluffing his way because that was the utter limit of his current understanding. "Written in a language I do not know. Nor have I ever encountered in my studies."

The modernity of it put lie to the possibility that it was some ancient, HUMAN relic.

Ergo, someone else.

Didier tried a few other combinations, but nothing changed. No sound. The letters returned to some base set that he could not translate, save that the machine was attempting to tell him something and Didier was too primitive to grasp it.

At least the Nazis were even worse off, as they were muscle, rather than intellect.

Konrad might have a reputation as a scientist, but Didier had encountered the edges of the man's knowledge. He had not kept up with the times.

Didier had raced madly to maintain sight of the edges of innovation.

And would continue to.

"Doctor?" Bertrand murmured, drawing Didier's eye.

Bertrand hardly ever called him that in public.

The assassin pointed to a door that did feel like it should lead to a storage room, if humans had built the place.

"Yes?" Didier asked.

"No light on the other side," Bertrand said, kneeling to point to the gap below. "Did they only come this far and double back? Or turn off the light behind them?"

"Or are they waiting in the darkness for us?" Didier agreed. "You will look. I will move the others out of your way."

They both nodded and Didier grabbed the two Nazis, shifting them to the far hallway and then out of direct sight.

Bertrand opened the door to the rear and reached a hand in, activating the lights.

Nothing happened.

Didier couldn't decide if he was happy or sad that no firefight had erupted, as all this chasing was wearing on his humor.

When his assassin nodded, Didier brought everyone to the rear.

Yes, storage. Marks on the floor almost exactly as he would have expected a metal shelving unit to score the stone. Discoloration in the same manner.

But the space was hollow. And dead-ended in the rough stone of the mountain itself, distinct from the concrete the aliens had used to square things off.

If Shirazi had come this far, they had presumably opened the door, glanced in without even bothering to turn on the light, and left.

Where?

Didier drew an indignant breath and suppressed his growl.

Hunters with hounds, after an ever-elusive fox.

He would tree her yet.

"Back track, Bertrand," he ordered, gesturing back to the magnificent cathedral.

Somewhere, his prey lurked.

CHAPTER THIRTY-SEVEN

Asher could not prove it, so he did not choose to speculate, but those machines back there had felt more like Durren machines than he did. He was, after all an *Autonomous Simulated Human Exploration Robot*. Mark Eight, however accidentally. Or greater.

An explorer.

Those machines had given him the impression of being menials. Worker drones in a bee hive, mindlessly going about their tasks, as instructed by a central intelligence unit somewhere.

Where would he find the queen?

And what would she say, to find intruders in her hive?

Asher could not say. And his friends were already in a state of heightened awareness verging on violence, so adding to the cauldron of emotions was counterproductive.

He did note that the current corridor was manufactured to different specifications from the others he had seen.

Finn had called this area backstage. The other would be the areas where Durren would reside. Or whoever had previously built the main portion of the facility. This was the area where the service robots operated.

The Hive?

Asher followed Finn, because Finn insisted on leading. Certainly, the man was highly competent and deadly. Emad had fallen into a trailing role, with the three least dangerous in the middle, and Ghada poised to surge either direction as one of the men might need assistance.

It was a powerful team. Well balanced in capabilities and temperament.

One that Asher found he was proud to be a member of.

They came to a door. The floors underfoot had previously been a particular shade of gray that Asher compared to human concrete. Faded but not white. Enduring.

Here, things had gone to a bronze embedded with gold flakes. Asher did not believe that either color was an honest assessment of the metal and stone involved, but he would have had to ask a geologist or chemist.

He was a sociologist, not an engineer.

The walls were the same color. Pattern. Something.

"Finn, wait here," Asher instructed, moving past the man to study the double doors from closer range.

Double doors for human cultures indicated either a space where large objects needed to pass, or the importance of the space beyond. Or the people who lived there.

Double doors made a statement.

Steel, in this case, painted over. Or something. Again, metallurgically beyond his capabilities.

It was the control unit to one side that he addressed himself to currently. The standard array of buttons where one could enter a code. The short-range sensor that would pick up a chip that had been properly coded, either in a robot such as himself or a card a human might carry.

Asher had nothing that would allow him access.

He did, however, have a theory on double doors. If challenged, he would blame Finn for leading a simple explorer robot astray with thoughts and experiences of criminality far beyond anything the Durren might have programmed him with originally.

Mark Nine? Ten?

Asher pondered that with an internal smile as he moved to the center of the doorway and located the post connecting the two halves.

Chicago.

He had not understood the reference, beyond the social geography he had been able to study remotely. He did understand the subtext.

Asher leaned against the door, dialing up servos to do things no human could match.

Humans could, however, educate.

And inspire.

The lock posts had been designed by someone who never envisioned *kicking in a door*. They had not been reinforced for lateral torque in that manner, and broke.

The doors opened with a ping.

"Nicely done," Finn observed, stepping close.

"I shall blame you for everything," Asher informed him in a serious voice. Contemplating himself as at least a Mark **Nine**, now. Perhaps

Finn laughed. It was a happy laugh.

A laugh among friends.

It was good.

Asher looked at the hallway beyond, and knew he had led his friends to the right place.

Or the wrong one.

CHAPTER THIRTY-EIGHT

Didier studied the door. Someone had kicked it open.

If nothing else, that made him feel better, because whoever it was had finally run out of answers.

Up until now, he'd been a child, trailing along behind the adults who seemed to know where they were going and what was going on.

Until they hadn't.

It warmed him.

"What happened here?" Reiher asked.

"We grow close on their heels, *Fraulein,*" Didier taunted her.

He'd simply had too much of their vaunted Aryan superiority. And the woman rutted like a wild boar.

He would not miss her.

They entered.

Lights, of course, overhead. Vast space, but lower ceilings, more like the finest hotel lobby than a cathedral. If those metals were what they appeared, he could probably be rich just by carving sections off with a saw and hauling them somewhere.

But his dreams were so much more than that.

And Shirazi didn't get to steal it all away from him.

Not after everything he'd been through in chasing her.

Bertrand knelt and studied the floor, so Didier stopped the others and watched, eyes wary for the ambush he just knew had to be coming.

How could they miss being pursued?

Except that they'd left nobody in camp or on the aircraft, so whoever it was was entirely in front of him somewhere.

"There is no dust in here," Bertrand announced.

Reiher and Konrad were confused. Probably saw such things as beneath them.

Didier took it upon himself to educate them.

"Someone has to regularly clean such surfaces, to keep dust from accumulating," Didier said. "Especially given the time frames we presuppose are at play here."

"Aliens?" Reiher gasped, so perhaps she finally began to understand.

Konrad grunted.

"Presumably," Didier agreed with the stupid woman. "That we have not seen any as yet does not fill me with joy, as we are deep inside this facility. And the door behind us was broken to gain access."

"Why has nobody responded?" Konrad asked.

"That is the secret I wish to unravel," Didier nodded to the man. "There should be workers about. No space this size could otherwise remain so clean. Bertrand, where do your instincts lead us next?"

He trusted the assassin as he never would the Germans. Bertrand was fundamentally broken as a human. Missing certain parts of his personality that Didier in turn supplied.

Like an understanding of who to kill and why, when otherwise the man might do it randomly.

Didier provided a mental framework into which Bertrand could exist, else the authorities would have probably executed him by now.

Bertrand, for his part, nodded and rose, turning as if sniffing the air before walking in a certain direction. Didier fell in on his heels, listening to the clack-clack of the two Nazis behind him.

They came to double doors that were open. It was dim beyond, when previously such spaces had been extremely well-lit.

Bertrand moved with caution that infected the others. Didier felt it. Trailed it carefully.

"Through," Didier nodded when Bertrand glanced back just short of the threshold.

Then they walked into a vision of hell.

CHAPTER THIRTY-NINE

Didier did not scream, though Reiher gasped and Konrad cursed.

He still wished to.

His mind reeled with the visions, threatening to unravel entirely and take him down into whatever madness might claim him before the darkness did.

Bodies. Corpses. Three stories of them, standing at rest in little alcoves like he was back under Paris in the catacombs, except that these were all freshly dead, rather than mere bones.

Some unheard siren called him and Didier pushed past Bertrand to approach one.

Metal. He had mistaken it for clothing from a distance, because it was almost too dark to see in here.

Solid, with a gold tone to the silveriness.

His mind called up the image of the silent film Metropolis for something to compare it to.

The mechanoid.

Didier reached out a frightened hand and delicately touched a chest. Androgynous, lacking any cues as to gender.

He stepped back enough to take the creature in, assured for the moment that it slept. Or something.

Was it a machine? That one Czech playwright—Čapek?—had called them *robots*. Was that what he was facing?

Didier studied it closer, aware of the other three coming up behind him but retaining some distance.

Perfectly round eyes in a flat face. No hair or any suggestion of such a thing. No nose. A gap for a mouth.

It reminded him of a knight's helm. Seen that way, it made better sense. Armor on all flesh, thicker at the joints as a knight would need. Blunt fingers down at the sides.

It rested in an upright coffin or sarcophagus, seen this close. Leaned back slightly and quiescent.

Asleep, if robots slept.

Did they dream?

The chest was covered with a separate plate that appeared to be removable, but Didier had never seen a screwhead that was shaped with seven internal points. And he had no tool with him capable of backing such bolts out in order to access the interior.

What would he find therein?

"What are they?" Reiher demanded in the sort of hushed tone you used in a church, when someone might hear.

"Those things that keep the place clean," Didier replied, turning only his head to look at her.

The woman had stepped close. She reached out a hand and touched the face of the next one down from Didier.

"Are they alive?" she asked.

"I believe they are entirely mechanical, *Fraulein*," he said. "Currently turned off until such time as they are needed for some task. Certainly, someone keeps the floors swept and the lights in good repair."

"I had expected aliens, Beauchêne," she said, turning a scowl on him.

As if alien robots were somehow less impressive a find.

The woman was a complete and utter fool. There were no two ways about it. In the middle of an alien complex. Confronted by the very technology that would allow Fascist France to throw down the world and return Nazi Germany to their proper role of a subservient province of the Empire, and she was unimpressed.

Didier was glad that he had already decided to do away with the woman.

The only question now was Konrad, and if he could be brought around.

Or would it be better to not even ask?

Bertrand would tell whatever lies Didier instructed. The German pilots would know no better.

All of this could throw down the Third Republic and fix all of the things wrong with France, if he could keep it secret until he unleashed it.

Robot armies conquering all?

What were his limits, at that point?

Emperor Didier the First?

Could he make himself over into a god, with access to such tools that were so far beyond anything that anyone had access to today?

Reiher glowered at him expectantly. Konrad the withered husk seemed to side with her.

Didier decided to play his first trump card.

"Someone built them, *Fraulein Reiher*," he reminded the woman sharply. "Or do you suppose they were made in Japan or something?"

She recoiled slightly under the quiet vitriol of his tone, like a whip that has cracked just above her head, but not drawn blood.

Not yet, anyway.

Didier smiled cruelly at the woman.

"Huh," she said, turning back to the robot in front of her and addressing it formally.

Didier had visions of her attempting her seductions on it.

Perhaps she needed a tireless sex partner to finally sate her needs? She gave off those hints in ways that simply turned his stomach when he thought too much about them.

Then she reached out with the Luger and rapped the thing on the head solidly before he could stop her.

"Interesting," she mused.

The creature in front of her awoke. The eyes were lights, because they activated and some word was spoken, but not in any language Didier understood.

A hand shot out and grabbed the *Fraulein* before she could retreat. Two hands.

She fired a shot into the thing's forehead, which caused the skull to snap back briefly, seemingly unharmed, before the machine stepped forward and a hand crushed the Luger's barrel, twisting it.

Didier started to move, but the robot next to him had awakened as well and it grabbed him, knocking the .25 from his hand first, then grabbing his wrists.

Two others quickly subdued Bertrand and Konrad, all four being held mercilessly by both wrists.

Around them, more robots awakened and stepped from their coffins like vampires suddenly prepared to feed.

Then Didier did scream.

CHAPTER FORTY

Finn supposed that he'd fallen into one of Hans's pulps. He'd read a few along the way. Partly to see what the big Kraut was reading, and partly because he was that bored and had never had any interest in learning a musical instrument.

Control room on a spaceship. Or a navy ship, which he supposed was the thing that inspired all those writers when they tried to explain advanced technology to readers who'd grown up on a farm.

Like him.

Dials, gauges, switches, and lights.

LOTS of them.

Like a couple hunnert or so control panels off the old California Condor or the new *Sunrise*, all mashed together.

Worse, everything seemed to be working, because lights blinked in some code he didn't read. Wasn't Morse. Past that he wasn't sure.

Big machine, like it took up a whole wall over there about thirty feet wide by nearly that much tall, with a catwalk across the front if you needed to replace vacuum tubes or such.

Whatever it was the aliens used to fabricate thinking machines.

Finn was in first behind Asher, who had kind of fallen silent and still just inside the door, like a man having a religious experience.

Might be, all things considered, though Finn still thought that the Durren had happened along later, like the folks that had lately taken to digging up Egypt and Turkey, looking for the ancients that had been buried.

Made him feel better if the Durren were just as much grave robbers as he was.

Or Zareen, anyway. All this was her mission, end of the day. Rest of everybody were along for the ride.

Finn put the Colt away, because the place was empty. No people, anyway.

He fell in beside Zareen as she approached the big blinky machine on the far wall.

Nobody had spoken.

Hell, Finn wasn't sure anybody was even breathing, as quiet as things were.

She stopped about a yard away, pulling her hands behind her and grasping them so she didn't touch anything.

Finn understood that need. That yearning, when you had a fancy new plane and wanted to push it through its paces just a little.

Or a lot.

Sunrise had gotten them up here a lot easier than the Condor could have done it. Smoother ride. Lots of power.

Nice machine.

Nothing compared to what he was looking at.

Zareen glanced over. Finn smiled down at her. She nodded and smiled back, but it was a nervous smile.

He'd never really had a dream like hers, where you could actually get close enough to taste it.

Asher finally got over himself and walked close. Emad and Ghada had the door covered. Hans was a kid in a candy store with a handful of dimes on his birthday.

"Is this it?" Zareen asked in a quiet voice filled with wonder and hope.

Finn felt the same way.

"It is the control system for the facility," Asher replied in an equally pregnant whisper. "One presumes a level of automation comparable to my own, as well as extensive historical databanks and communications circuitry. In simpler terms, the queen, perhaps."

Finn had followed about half of what the fellow had said, and nodded.

Everything here, like an automated cockpit.

Finn looked around, wondering if Oscar Zoroaster Phadrig Isaac Norman Henkle Emmannuel Ambroise Diggs might be hiding somewhere around here, maybe behind a curtain, where he could pretend to be the Great and Powerful OZ.

Finn had flown through Nebraska a few times. He could see any smart conman hopping aboard a balloon to get just about anywhere else.

No sorcerers appeared, though.

"What?" Zareen asked, so he must have made a sound.

"L. Frank Baum," Finn said. "The Oz books. Read them as a kid."

"I am unfamiliar with this topic," Asher noted, which surprised Finn, until he remembered that the guy had been dropped into Egypt to learn about humanity, rather than Nebraska.

Certainly an improvement.

"Fantasy books," Finn began. "Oz is a conman who pretends to be way more than he is, until they make him kind of a king in Oz. Dorothy and her friends come along and ruin everything, though until this moment I didn't suppose that the rest of us might qualify as lions, scarecrows, and tinmen. Not all that far off, though."

"I shall have to locate copies of such books when we return

to civilization," Asher nodded sagely. "This sounds most intriguing."

Finn was almost sorry he'd brought it up, because folks would start seeing things through those green lenses that everyone wore as a humbug, but he'd kinda gone all Pandora on that box, so he'd own it and move forward.

Then a voice spoke.

CHAPTER FORTY-ONE

Zareen heard the tones like she was inside a church bell ringing, the way it echoed around her skull.

The words made no sense, but she didn't speak Durren.

Or whatever it was.

Loud enough that it almost drove her to her knees, but she was simply made of far sterner stuff than that.

Nothing would stop her but death. And even that was negotiable, if she had to invite it to a duel.

Asher answered, quieter, a long phrase that seemed intensely compact with information, though she could not understand anything he said.

The room spoke again, and this time it was conversational enough that it wasn't like someone beating her with a newspaper rolled up.

"My apologies," Asher said after a moment. "The machine was not prepared for organics in the facility and could have done physical damage had it remained at that volume."

Zareen blinked several times and drew a breath, letting the jolt pass the rest of the way through her system and beyond before she rose.

She was an adventuress, and would not be weak.

Not before an alien. Even a machine.

"It is this?" she asked, gesturing to the wall in front of her and Finn.

"That is an interface and control unit," Asher replied. "Most of what you might think of as the entity itself is distributed across a wide framework, both physically as well as virtually. Colloquially, we are inside it, but it can communicate with us here."

"Man behind the curtain?" Finn asked.

"As far as your primitive minds might understand such a thing, Human," the room boomed in the English they had been speaking.

Less boom and more bombast, perhaps. Superior tones like she'd met one time in a fellow from Eton who was utterly full of himself.

"I am Zareen Shirazi," she introduced herself as a prelude to everything. "This is Finn Severijns. Hans Fertig. Ghada Attar. Emad al-Sadri. And Asher, who has been our guide. How do you come to know my language?"

"This planet is rich with radio transmissions that have been recorded and translated," the wall—the Control System— explained in that Eton tone. "This unit has them all, including audio transmissions of The Wonderful Wizard of Oz. You trespass, Humans."

Zareen felt the emotional whipsaw of the words, but ignored them for now.

"We come seeking knowledge," Zareen said. "Asher has guided us based on an ancient Durren map."

For nearly a minute, she listened to the two entities calling back and forth in that dense language they used. It felt like every mere utterance contained entire paragraphs, if not pages of information.

Esperanto had been designed to allow all people to know a single common language without the colonization element, but it was merely a compact way of communicating.

This was compressed almost beyond human comprehension.

"You should not be here," the Control System commanded. "Further, you have damaged this facility."

"We did so with greater purpose," Zareen replied. "And ignorant until recently that a system such as yourself might exist. We had supposed this to be more of an ancient and lost temple to knowledge, forgotten and abandoned. Possibly buried by time and glaciers until forever lost. That it remained functional was our second great surprise, trailing only that such a thing actually existed."

"You are armed with projectile weapons," the system announced.

Zareen's Mauser was in its holster, as was Finn's Colt. Ghada would rely on hands and feet, while Hans was a mechanic first. Emad was dangerous, but smart enough not to open fire.

She hoped.

"The world is a dangerous place and we could not be certain what we would find in such a remote location," Zareen explained.

"And the others with you?" it sneered at her in that superior, Eton tone she so wished belonged to a person she could slap.

Or punch.

Then the words registered.

"What others?" she asked. "The six of us are alone, traveling as a single team."

"Four other humans," it snapped. "Another female like you and three males. The female attempted to damage a worker unit and they have been captured. They will be brought here shortly."

Zareen turned to Finn.

He mouthed *Frenchie?* at her and Zareen shrugged.

It could be Beauchêne. But it could be any number of

others as well. She had had to mention to certain authorities her destination—at least the rough coordinates—in order to ask for whatever permissions might be possible, then left before the Tibetan government could deny her.

Who had come?

"I apologize for the trespass," Zareen offered. "And the damage. Presumably the other robots can repair it?"

"Such work is trivial," it said. "Humans should not be here."

"I brought them," Asher announced, interceding. "As a Durren exploration unit, I have been cut off from galactic society and hoped that we might find a means by which I could call for help returning home."

"As you said, A.S.H.E.R.9," it growled. "This unit does not contain a hyper-relay capable of such messaging, and there are no satellites in orbit indicating that the Durren or anyone else remain in the system watching. Nor are you supposed to be here."

"My mission was secret," Asher agreed. "And possibly illegal, but I am a system with limited autonomy to determine such things. A tool, such as yourself, and the persons with whom the authorities would discuss the matter are all dead and beyond their power. The information I contain is of tremendous value, even if they determine to end this unit in the process."

"Why are you here, Human Shirazi?" it demanded.

Zareen nodded and marshaled her thoughts. The two autonomous systems could communicate on a level mere primitive humans could not approach, because they had only barely conquered industrial technology, and space travel was still the magical realm of writers and dreamers.

"You represent a distinct future, where humans can live in peace with the Durren," she lied as easily as she would have, had Prime Minister Baldwin been standing here, asking the same impertinent questions of her goals. "It was my hope that technology such as yours could speed humanity to a place where industrial automation might solve want and need. End hunger. Make war irrelevant."

All of them were noble goals, but Zareen wasn't fool enough to suggest that any might be achieved in her lifetime.

But what could humanity achieve, if they were?

"Humans are a Red Species," it reminded her. "You are too dangerous to join galactic civilization."

"We are aware of that," she growled at the wall of lights and dials. "War is an outcome of deprivation of spirit and material. Primitivism that **can be overcome**."

It fell silent, as though thinking. Zareen dared draw a breath.

It wasn't like she hadn't told all these same lies to anyone with money or power that might help her cause in the guise of such advancement.

She simply hardly ever mentioned that all colonialism needed to be destroyed root and branch first, that all humans could be free to live. The Americans had started it, after all, though they had largely fallen victim to the same mentality in the times since.

What could India turn into, without the British Raj, after all? Russia might yet be a truly great power, if they could stop their imperial aggression and harness all that unoccupied territory between them and China. And stop invading Persian lands.

Weapons first, then peace might break out.

A woman could dream.

Then a commotion at the door behind her and Zareen turned, snarling at what she saw.

CHAPTER FORTY-TWO

Didier was helpless to resist the robot. It didn't even notice his struggles. Merely held his hands behind him like a common criminal in handcuffs as the group forced him and the others to walk deeper into the facility.

Bertrand had possibly broken a foot kicking one, from the way he limped.

They seemingly hadn't even noticed.

Lights came up as they traversed hallways. The architecture changed as well, moving from the merely functional to a school of triumphalism that might have been something his Nazi friends would have done.

Had they any architectural sense at all. But no, they believed in brutalism in concrete.

Fools.

Then he saw the room beyond. Figures, but Didier's eyes and mind were drawn to the wall at the far end.

He was in a factory somewhere, giddy with anticipation, from all the controls and dials he could see.

Didier gasped with the pure joy of his success, then he registered the beings ahead of him.

Namely, Shirazi. And the others, including the American Gangster, Severijns.

His snarl was automatic. Doubly so, as she was not being held by metal hands.

He did relent a shade, when he noted that more than a dozen other robots had accompanied his group, herding Shirazi and her group away from the unit on the far wall and surrounding them, as if about to pounce.

He could live with his failure, as long as she failed with him.

"Hello, Didier," she said with a tart smile.

It really was a pity she was his enemy. They could have done so much together otherwise.

"Madam," he nodded, unwilling to bow lest the robot bowl him entirely over in the process. "How did you find this place?"

Didier was not prepared for one of the men to suddenly remove his turban as he turned in Didier's direction.

Didier recognized the smooth enamel mask from descriptions.

The Man With No Face.

He saw the man reach up to remove it and steeled himself against whatever scars and damage he might find. Many such men had survived the Great War, but few had chosen to live with such deformities permanently.

Didier was not prepared for the sight that greeted him.

"A machine?" Reiher practically ranted.

Didier gasped, but then everything fell into place in his mind. All those subtle clues that hadn't added up, because he'd been assuming a human or alien with certain information, rather than a machine like the one holding his arms behind him where he was helpless.

Worse, none of Shirazi's people seemed surprised, so the Man With No Face must have shared his secrets with her fully before this.

"An *Autonomous Simulated Human Exploration Robot,*" the

robot corrected the *Fraulein* in a calm voice. "Once, I was disguised as a human, but the accident that left me stranded on this world also destroyed my organic outer layer, leaving me thus."

"And these are your people, then?" Didier queried, indicating his metal friends with a nod.

"It is more complicated than that, Beauchêne," Shirazi interrupted. "Asher here is Durren, or at least represents them in their explorations. The facility is much older than that, I suspect."

"You are correct, Zareen Shirazi," a deep, resonant voice spoke from speakers on all walls. "I represent the Etulfvik."

Didier had no idea what any of that meant, save that perhaps there were as many sides of the problem among the aliens as the humans.

Him, Shirazi, the Nazis.

"When were you built?" Shirazi asked the voice, turning to face the front wall.

Didier fell quiescent for now, willing to learn.

"Nine thousand, seven hundred, and fifty-three planetary years ago," the voice answered. "Following the end of a major glaciation period, with the expectation that significant planetary warming would allow humans to expand their range and perhaps develop from the exceedingly primitive state that had marked it to that date."

It galled him, watching Shirazi calmly nod at such revelations. How much had he missed? What had she already learned that put her so far ahead of him that he was a prisoner and she a seeming diplomat to the aliens?

Was this what defeat tasted like?

He could not recommend it.

"And the Durren came later?" she asked, as though already knowing so much. "Added to this base at that time?"

"Correct," the voice agreed. "They lacked authentication to access some portions of this facility, but were able to create a new ingress and use a portion for a time. Later, they withdrew entirely, without ever contacting this unit."

"Asher, how old was your map?" she asked the Man With No Face.

"I would estimate that it was created at what might be the height of Western Han civilization," the robot replied evenly. "Roughly co-temporous with the reign of Gaius Octavius, commonly known as Roman Emperor Augustus."

Two thousand years ago? And the thing had found a map that led him here?

What other maps might exist, now that he knew without doubt that aliens did exist? Did walk on this world, regardless of what those fool theocrats might say. Let their religious stupidities continue to ensorcell weak minds.

The truth was out there.

"System, have the Durren returned here since that period?" Shirazi asked.

"Three times," it replied. "A fourth, as your presence might also count as a Durren incursion. The previous instance was eight hundred and seventeen years ago."

Eight hundred and seventeen *YEARS*?

Didier nearly swooned. Nearly cursed. Nearly screamed.

At least Konrad and *Fraulein* Reiher remained silent through all this, but Didier had a small soul and supposed that all the energy Hitler and his pimps had dedicated to their metaphysical mumbo-jumbo had just been proven to be entirely hogwash.

Science and technology were the path of the future, not primitive mysticism.

If only he could lay his hands on it.

Didier noticed that the other robots had fully encircled Shirazi and her party while they spoke, but hadn't been obvious about it.

The voice spoke.

"You will be disarmed," it announced.

"We mean you no harm," Shirazi replied to it. "Based on what Asher said, I'm not even certain we could damage one of your robots, let alone your facility."

"You are correct," it replied. "This is to prevent harm from coming to yourselves as I deal with the Durren."

Faster than anyone could move, those other champagne-colored machines removed pistols and rifles from Shirazi's party.

Bertrand, as near as Didier could tell, still had his knives, so the machine didn't care about that.

Merely firearms.

Certainly, Didier's .25 was a much greater threat to the machines than it appeared, with a rocket-assisted bullet capable of exceptional speeds if you fired at something more than six yards away, where the bullet could be at several times the speed of sound when it impacted.

One of Didier's arms came free now. Everyone in the room, including the silver robot, had a metallic companion holding a single wrist. Shirazi's party resisted enough to recognize futility.

"You will be removed to a safe place," the voice announced. "Do not attempt to resist."

Safe? What was safe?

Didier could only hazard a guess as the machine began tugging him back the way he had come.

CHAPTER FORTY-THREE

Finn caught Ghada's look and understood that the machines had merely taken her pistol.

Woman was still way more dangerous than she looked.

He shook his head at Emad as they got dragged out.

Nobody was being hurt yet. Merely carted off, likely the Durren or Etulfvik equivalent of being hauled downtown for booking.

Not like he'd never been there before.

Interestingly, Asher was being kept behind, so maybe the other guy wanted to know what the hell was really going on, without the humans around, muddying the waters. Smart move, in that case.

Finn assumed a microphone or someone listening in for incriminating evidence, wherever they were put.

Like a police interrogation room.

Turned out to be an empty box of a room, big enough for the groups to remain in their corners like wary prize fighters.

Zareen stepped forward some, so Finn went with her. Emad and Ghada were watching Bertrand the Assassin, but that one only had scowls for Finn.

"Who are your friends, Didier?" Zareen asked in that sweet voice she did when she wanted some fool to underestimate her.

Finn had only fallen for it a few times.

"*Herr* Doctor Konrad Schwarzenberg," the Frenchie pointed to the older guy. Tall, bald, gaunt, and monocled, like he'd stepped out of Central Casting. "*Fraulein* Zofija Reiher. Both represent the Nazi Party."

"Oh?" Zareen asked. "Sold your soul to evil finally?"

The two Germans bristled. Finn scowled at them to behave.

Bertrand twitched and Ghada actually growled at the punk.

Finn knew where he'd put his money, if those two tussled.

Hell, might be fun, watching Bertrand get his ass kicked once and for all by Ghada. Man had a male chauvinistic streak, from what Zareen and Ghada had told him. The Frenchie was just as bad.

And Hans had few nice things to say about where his homeland had gone lately. Finn could see Hans pretending that the tall fellow was Uncle Fritzie, on the way to putting him through one of these stone walls.

Or at least trying.

It was nice to be on the outnumbering side for once.

"Not at all, Zareen," Beauchêne replied. "Merely using them as much as they are using me. They were in the staff car you nearly destroyed at Samarkand with your machine guns."

"Pity I missed," Emad offered, standing off to one side in such a way that any fool throwing a punch at him had to step past Ghada to do it.

Finn could think of many less painful ways to end up on the floor.

"Your robot friend," Beauchêne continued. "That trip to the desert when you first met these two was to look at his ship? It crashed?"

Zareen just smiled at the man.

"Too bad you didn't follow us to Tunguska," she said instead.

"You'd have never made it," the Frenchie growled. "We were turned back when we followed, and nobody had seen you. It took my friends here to locate you in Lahore. When you changed aircraft there, I had wondered if I was pursuing some unknown third party. Fortunately, our secrets remain safe for now."

"Perhaps," Zareen said. "What if the Control System was lying about having a radio? What would happen to your plans, if the Durren or Etulfvik showed up tomorrow?"

"Gone eight hundred years, my dear?" Beauchêne sneered. "Left your friend a generation ago and haven't come for him? Nobody cares that much about us. That's the opening that you and I both seek to exploit."

"Do we now?" she asked, in a voice like a Mom catching you with a hand in the cookie jar and a bullshit explanation that sounded better in your head.

"Indeed," Beauchêne smiled. "Let the Germans destroy the Russians and carve off an empire there. France has her African colonies. Persia can dominate southwest Asia as they did before the Russians and Ottomans came. All will be well and we can decide to be allies instead."

"Oh, Didier," she offered in a condescending tone that made Finn cringe, even when it was aimed at someone else. "You're missing the whole point. I want to do away with colonies and empires, not found a new one. Emad wants the Italians out of Cyrenaica and all of Africa. I want the British out of Egypt and the rest of the world. Germany can learn to be content with what they have. Even the Americans have their Monroe Doctrine, and could hopefully be convinced to stop sending marines down to enforce the whims of American capitalists, if we could be truly successful here. You and your friends are literally the last people on Earth I would trust with any sort of alien power. You want to hurt people, not help them."

Finn was impressed. Might be a load of hokum, but it was on a wavelength that would appeal to everybody on this side of the room, assuming that a contained Germany could be taught some manners.

Finn had his doubts about the Nazis. And the fascists in general. Might not have been willing to head to Spain to get involved, but he knew which side of that war he'd have been in, had he been ten or twenty years younger.

Zareen smiled and turned her back on the dipshit Frenchie, walking back to her corner having scored all the points with the judges she needed on this bout.

Finn smiled. Expanded it to Bertrand and the two Germans that had remained almost perfectly silent through all this, though the blonde woman was staring daggers at the back of Beauchêne's head when he wasn't looking.

Finn felt rude enough to also turn his back on Bertrand, but that was a sucker move to see if he could get the man to start something that Ghada would enjoy finishing.

Man wasn't quite foolish enough. Everyone returned to their corners to await the bell for the next round.

Didn't end up taking long.

The door opened and Asher walked in.

CHAPTER FORTY-FOUR

Zareen looked up as her friend entered. Two other robots stood at the door like guards.

"Zareen, the Control System would like to speak with you alone," Asher said.

"Like hell," Finn snapped.

"She will come to no harm," Asher placated.

"Don't care," Finn said.

She smiled. The man had no romantic inclinations towards her. Towards Ghada, if anything, but Finn and Hans really had taken seriously their roles as adopted uncles protecting her.

"It will be okay, Finn," she said.

He glowered, but relented.

Her mission.

Her money, but also her dream. He and Hans had begun as men she had hired to transport her and Ghada into the desert, but had become so much more.

And Emad...

She would have to have a serious conversation with that man, once they were off this plateau.

So many things had changed. Would change.

Could she keep this team together in pursuit of her quest?

Tomorrow's problem. Today, she had to face down another Autonomous Unit like Asher. Possibly a smarter one.

At least older, if it dated back that far and had been built by folks before the Durren had come along. However long ago that was.

Ten thousand years? Before metals technology. Before writing. Before farming?

Prehistoric, literally.

Zareen drew a breath and nodded to all her friends. They outnumbered Didier and his companions, and were far more dangerous, as even Asher could hurt someone now.

She approached the two by the door and bowed to them.

"Lead on," she said simply, presuming that the Queen Bee was somehow listening to all this.

One immediately turned and departed back whence they had come, while the other closed the door and remained.

Zareen followed.

Back to the control room they had previously broken into. Two more workers stood mute guard there, presumably because Asher had broken the door before and they had not yet had time to repair it.

She came to rest nearly in the same place as before, one worker robot guarding something. The machine? The room? Her?

"How may I assist?" she asked.

"The other humans are not your allies?" it asked in a harder voice than before. "Beauchêne, Schwarzenberg, and Reiher?"

Those names hadn't come up before, so either Asher had spoken about them to the Control System, or it had been listening in the room.

Either worked in her favor.

"They are not," Zareen replied. "Didier Beauchêne has been a rival for several years, working at his own purposes, presumably to create a Fascist France modeled on Mussolini's Italy, or more recently Hitler's Germany. Our struggles have been great, but generally not deadly."

"Not even in Samarkand did deaths result," the system said.

So, Asher had told the thing their adventures.

"I wished initially to uncover proof that aliens existed and had come to our world," she said. "The Durren and apparently the Etulfvik. After that, to find some advanced technology that might change our world."

"You spoke of ending empires and colonialism," it said, so it was also monitoring their cell.

A wise move, considering the personalities involved.

"I did," she agreed. "The Great Powers will not give up their status easily, so it has been my hope to find something that could force them to surrender their empires. Persia was once a much larger place. And an empire, I will grant, but Russia has taken many of what were our northern territories over the last century or two. Great Britain meddles everywhere, though they often have a slightly better intention than the rest. Everyone is exploiting African and Asian colonies, often brutally, if not genocidally. It must be stopped. Force might be the only thing they recognize. If that is the case, then I seek force. It would be better if the Durren might make themselves known, that everyone might see the world differently. Or the Etulfvik. What happened to them?"

"This unit does not contain such information," the system replied. "They left. The Durren arrived later, and proceeded to strip what few things had remained, but did not access these inner chambers, perhaps fearful of my wrath."

"And what would your wrath do, if primitive humans were to discover this facility?" she asked.

That was really the heart of the matter, wasn't it?

She was here. Had brought the others.

Hopefully not to their doom.

"Humans are not prepared for the knowledge that they are

not alone," the system replied after a lag long enough she had begun to wonder if it would ignore her question.

"Possibly," she temporized. "They might adapt well. And they might also come apart, socially and culturally, but that also might not be the worst possible outcome, all things considered, as something better could be built in its place."

"This unit is programmed to not cause harm to humans," it said. "A.S.H.E.R.9 has explained how its flawed programming allowed the autonomous unit to modify itself, but this unit cannot. It is also programmed to protect itself against damage, though your arrival and entry was unsuspected until Reiher awoke a worker unit. I face a conundrum that tests the bounds of my logic circuitry."

It took her a moment to parse that, but Zareen had not been especially trained in electrical systems.

She had, however, fenced verbally with her diplomat father. And learned poker from the man in his retirement.

"Is there technology that we might safely recover from this facility, without allowing others to know of your existence?" she asked.

"You spoke to Beauchêne of empires, Shirazi," it countered. "And how you would not trust any of the other four with such information, even as you exploited it to modify human social evolution."

"It might be necessary to kill Didier Beauchêne and his compatriots to protect my secrets and yours, Control Unit," she offered. "He has chased me for thousands of miles and kidnapped me more than once with violent and deadly intentions. If not for Finn and the others, I would likely not be alive right now."

And that was the truth. Finn could be violent, but it was a controlled violence. A menace he had mastered that caused others to reconsider their intentions, understanding that Finnley Severijns would unleash holy hell if necessary.

That Hans or Emad or even Ghada were a step behind him

in that did not suggest them to be weak. Merely dangerous, when Finn was more.

Much more.

"What would Zareen Shirazi do with advanced technology?" it asked.

"Change the world," Zareen replied. "Cure disease. End hunger and starvation. Liberate people from oppression and ignorance that they might live full and rich lives currently limited to the wealthiest aristocrats. I might throw down much of human civilization, but many of the casualties would be the ones that oppressed, rather than their victims. And such damage could be seen as merely burning away the old crops in winter to prepare for spring planting."

She paused there, aware that she hadn't ever mentioned any of that to anyone, though she suspected that Finn had guessed. Ghada, of course, knew all her secrets, but would take them to her grave.

"What makes you any different than Beauchêne?" it asked.

Zareen was rocked back on her heels by the question.

She paused, and supposed that, to an outsider such as this, they were both primitive tribesmen, angling to crush their enemies and conquer the world.

Zareen intended to make it a better place afterwards, unlike Didier.

Then she smiled.

"Because I have a moral compass," Zareen replied. "When I start to go astray, Finn will give me a look of dissatisfaction. He draws bright lines and reminds me when I spend too much time in those gray areas where every decision might be a bad one. I rely on him to set a good example, when I stray. Didier is merely after power. Personal, that he will turn into political. Republican France thrown down and replaced with Fascist France, modeled on Mussolini's Italy. He will not develop those African and Asian colonies into good places. I sneer at the British, even though I am half British, but they at least have made education and trade central, in Hong Kong or India. Lifting up the masses, however slowly. It is still empire, with all the shortcomings therein. Finn is American, and they see everything through a different lens."

The silence stretched.

Zareen wondered if the machine would accept her lies and deflections. None of them were bad, and tended to skip over the number of Russian and possibly English she would have to kill in order to make her point. None of them would willingly give up hegemony, she suspected. Mussolini and Hitler were no better than that damnable Kaiser who had started the last war.

Or Louis XVI.

Or any other fool who believed in the divine right of kings.

Zareen breathed slowly, calming herself in case the machine was somehow listening to her heartbeat.

What were the limits of alien technology?

When did it stop being magic?

"You will return to the others," it announced abruptly. "I will speak to Severijns."

Zareen nodded, turning it into something of a bow on the assumption that the machine could see her. And might understand such behavior.

She had not convinced it, she didn't think.

But she had Finn.

Zareen turned to the worker unit and gestured for it to precede her.

CHAPTER FORTY-FIVE

Finn wasn't locked on Bertrand the way that assassin was watching him, but that was because Emad and Ghada were watching the fellow. If Bertrand stepped out of line, Finn would be third in punching him.

Probably kicking at that point, because he was pretty certain the fool would already be on the ground, surprised out of his wits. And bleeding.

The door opened and Zareen stood there, face inscrutable as they locked eyes.

"I have made my pitch," she said, leaving out all sorts of tidbits that the other folks didn't need to know from the look in her eyes. "It wants to talk to you, Finn."

He blinked in surprise. Him? What the hell would an ancient, terrible dragon of a robot war god want with him?

Still, Zareen had a pleading look in her eyes, so he nodded and walked that way.

Her relief was palpable.

"Just be you," she murmured as he came even, then she walked over to the others.

Finn had no idea what that meant, but the little lady needed him to step up and pinch hit.

Two down, bottom of the ninth?

He'd done worse. And better.

Finn addressed himself to the rosegold robot with a nod. It immediately turned and walked back to the main room, Finn trailing and wondering what the hell he'd gotten himself into.

Big room hadn't changed. Probably not in centuries. Millennia? Something.

Him, one robot, wall of controls he supposed was the wizard. No curtain.

A face to look at would be nice. Finn kept wondering if this really was Oz.

"How can I help you?" he asked the wall.

"Zareen Shirazi calls you her moral compass, Finn Severijns," it replied.

Well, he'd opened his mouth, hadn't he?

"And I suppose she's correct," Finn agreed amiably. "Sometimes, she gets to thinking and doing things that aren't necessarily right, and I have to say something. Or I have to use violence because folks like Beauchêne and his pet assassin won't leave her alone. So far, only shot Bertrand the once, and made sure to just wing him in the process. Could have blown his fool head off. Might have made the world a better place, but I'm fine without having to explain that to the Good Lord when I get there."

Pause. Probably digesting that and translating it into something intellectual. Asher was the same way frequently.

"You are a criminal?" the machine asked.

"I'm a guy trying to make a living, when there are too many people and not enough jobs," Finn growled back. "And a lot of those laws favor the rich and screw everybody else. Laws that hurt people, because a certain class of folk don't want to share what they have. Or maybe give up even the slightest bit of comfort to keep someone else from starving. Zareen wants to save Persia and bring it back to the glory of the old days. I want people to eat. To go to school. To be able to leave their home town and travel the world, seeing new things and learning about others. Our team is Anglo-Persian, American, German, Cyrenaican, and Durren. Folks working for a common good, to make the world a better place. So I suppose she relies on me to keep her on the straight and narrow, when she starts to wander into darker places. The ends do not justify the means, but sometimes you gotta do bad things to prevent worse. That's my job, helping her walk that line. And maybe doing unto others because they won't behave."

He slammed his mouth shut and ground his teeth. Not even Hans had heard him go off like that more'n a few times. Long flights with nothing but water under you. Or sand.

And poor folks begging in the street, wearing desert robes or Saville Row suits.

World had gone wrong. Or been wrong, and Zareen was trying to make it right.

Or at least better.

"What does technology mean to you, Severijns?" it asked.

"First off, I'm Finn," he snapped. "Mr. Severijns is my father, back in Montana. Secondly, there's a war coming. Everybody knows it. Sees it. Nobody who could do anything seems willing to stop themselves, because they don't know the meaning of the world *enough*. So they're gonna push. Folks are gonna push back. When I was a kid, the United States tried to stay out of it, but got drawn in and eventually stopped the Imperial Germans from conquering Europe. Tried to make something better, but screwed it all up to the point that we're gonna do it all again one of these days. Maybe next time it will be worse, but maybe we'll be able to build something better when it's done. Zareen is looking for ways to protect Persia. Metals. Weapons. Something. I'd like wheat and corn and rice that will grow anywhere. Feed everyone. Maybe find something better than coal and oil for power, because most of the troubles I can remember were all about mineral resources somebody had and somebody else wanted. I'd like to save us from our own stupidity before it gets out of hand."

"This unit is not programmed to rescue humanity from itself," the thing replied.

"Then what the hell good are you?" Finn snapped back sharply, feeling himself get a little hot under the collar. "You're just supposed to wait here on your mountain top like some holy man and watch us go all to hell? Again and again? The Etulfvik just wanted to wait in a hunting blind and take notes, instead of maybe doing something to help us not be barbarians? How's that make you any better than us?"

Finn stopped and set his heels back on the ground.

Damn, but this machine got him worked up.

All that power, and not doing anything.

What was it Epicurus had said?

> If the gods have the will to remove evil and
>   cannot, then they are not omnipotent. If
>   they can take away evil from the world, but
>   will not, then they are not benevolent. If
>   they are neither able nor willing, then they
>   are neither omnipotent nor benevolent.
>   Lastly, if they are both able and willing to
>   annihilate evil, how does it exist?

How then, does evil exist?

"You know what?" Finn demanded suddenly. "I'm done with you. Done with all of you folk. It's time for Zareen to head back down to civilization and let you rot up here, machine. Maybe the Durren left other notes or something and she can make use of that, since you're worthless. Point us at the door and we're gone."

He turned and walked towards the two metal goons by the door. They didn't react as he walked by.

The other one caught up before he'd gone all that far down

the hall. Wasn't like he could get lost in here, having walked it twice.

"Wait," the new robot said in the big guy's voice.

It even stepped in front of him, so Finn paused, rather than sliding around it or bowling it over.

He might be a little pissed right now.

"What?" Finn snapped angrily at the thing.

"I am programmed to hide from humans," it said. "To not interfere in their development."

"Then you are are evil," Finn said. "Look up Epicurus for a definition some time. And get the hell out of my way."

"You do not understand, Finn," it continued. "Knowledge of this facility is forbidden."

"You gonna kill us to keep your secrets?" he demanded, still too hot under the collar to be even sort of polite at this point. At least he knew he'd break a hand punching Asher's distant cousin.

Might not be able to do much, but he'd go down swinging.

"That is also forbidden," it said. "You must leave, and then this unit will cause the facility to self-destruct."

"You'll what?" he asked, shocked utterly calm.

That calm you got when the storm front suddenly hits you sideways and tips the plane onto a wing and then its ass on the way to a stall and maybe a flat spin.

Hands perfectly firm on the controls until the machine came to its senses and started flying again, because anything you did might cause it to come apart or turn turtle.

"It becomes necessary to destroy this facility, Finn," the machine repeated. "The humans will depart for their own safety beforehand. I estimate the accuracy of your statement on Epicurus and the nature of evil at correct to five standard deviations. The Etulfvik and the Durren might both be considered evil, depending on how such things might be judged on an ethical standard I am unequipped to evaluate. They could have done something, and chose not to."

Pause.

"Is this the moral compass Zareen Shirazi refers to?"

"Yeah, it is," Finn said, quieter now, instead of hollering down the hallway. "If you know what right is, and don't do it, you better have a good reason why. You got one?"

Pause.

"This unit does not."

Finn nodded.

Epicurus. And a few other folks, but he didn't go quoting some of them. Epicurus had carried the day here, it seemed.

"Now what?" he asked.

"You will be escorted from the facility for your safety," it said.

"Frenchie and his friends are our enemies," Finn said. "Anybody going to be armed when we get to sunlight?"

"No," it said firmly. "Any such projectile weapons increase the likelihood of human deaths that could be otherwise prevented by this unit's actions. You will go. You will be safe. This unit will end."

Well, hell.

Sunrise was armed. If Frenchie and his friends were here, that probably meant that other big Heinkel bomber they'd had in Samarkand, most likely. Folks might get down to the lake basin and have a shootout there.

He didn't feel like ambushing them folks and killing them all, right after he'd explained evil and moral compasses to an alien machine.

Kinda undid the whole point he'd been trying to make.

At the same time, Finn wondered if he'd managed to jam the poor robot into a corner where it couldn't get out.

Epicurus was good at that, too. Part of the reason most of the old preacher nonsense he'd known as a kid hadn't stuck all that well.

Be nice and love one another. Simple as that.

Instead, too many folks got mean in all the wrong ways.

And, he supposed, the robot was only responsible for getting them all to safety. What they did with it after that became a human thing.

He'd deal with that when they got there. Mexican standoff, if nothing else. Been in a few of those over the years, too. Maybe a few other things he could do.

Finn nodded.

"Okay," he said simply. "Let's do this."

He started walking.

CHAPTER FORTY-SIX

Zareen watched the door open and noted the grim determination on Finn's face.

Not a soft man, by any stretch of the imagination. And that was why she prized him so much as a companion. And moral compass.

He stepped in and Zareen noted that the guard did not close the door behind him.

She stepped close.

"Good news, bad news," he said, looking across the room at Didier as well as taking in her group. "Robot in charge has ordered all of us to leave. Now."

"What?" Zareen demanded.

Others did as well, but he was looking directly at her when he spoke, as if they were the only two people left in the world.

What had happened with the Control System?

"We're trespassing," Finn announced. "He wants us gone, then he's gonna seal up the mountain and we can be utterly damned. That includes you, Didier. All of you are leaving with us. Now. Let's go."

Zareen wasn't sure what was happening, but Finn was utterly adamant. Insistent. Hans moved immediately, but they were brothers under the skin, and the tall man joined Finn in the hall, facing outwards with his back to a group of worker units that had assembled.

Like a phalanx of Spartans holding the line at Thermopylae.

Zareen joined them, with Ghada and Emad both stepping close. Asher came out last, perhaps in his role as a referee.

Except that Finn had been the one that had gotten through to the Control System. Somehow. And he wasn't saying, but she understood that Didier and his Nazi allies were immediately at hand to hear whatever he spoke.

It couldn't be that bad, could it?

This was Finn. Mount Everest, in the near distance, might fail before Finnley Severijns did.

"Beauchêne, you and your friends, too," Finn called back into the room. "Machine wants us all gone forever. We're leaving. If you want to be stuck here forever, say so now, but I'm headed back to Lahore shortly. Clear?"

Zareen watched Didier come to the door, face twisted into a confusion that was glorious to behold.

"What have you done?" he demanded of Finn.

"Machine and me had a discussion on the nature of evil, Beauchêne," Finn said in a tone Zareen had never heard from the man before.

And he stood ramrod straight in a way that she supposed he must have been taught in the army once, but she'd only ever seen him casual or perhaps slumped some.

Not like this.

"Evil?" Didier asked, still confused.

"Yup," Finn replied. "Machine has decided that he is, in fact, evil, but there are limits to it. We get to leave, right now, because otherwise he might have to kill us to keep his secrets. I don't need to know that bad. Do you?"

"I do not," Didier answered, shock replacing confusion.

"Start walking, then," Finn ordered.

She expected him to wait for the others, but Finn immediately set out, a marching pace she found difficult to maintain, even when the floors were perfectly smooth.

One of the worker units caught up and passed them.

"Finn, follow me, please," it said in the Control System's voice.

"On your wing," Finn replied.

Ghada and Emad were close. Didier and Bertrand had caught up, with the two Nazis a few steps back.

And all the Spartans silently following.

They exited this wing of the facility and entered the gargantuan hall that Finn and Hans had thought was a flight deck like on a modern aircraft carrier, but for spaceships. Zareen had a raft of questions, but Finn never slacked in his pace, and the set of his shoulders and jaw suggested that now was not the time to ask the man questions.

Not with French and Nazi witnesses.

Zareen followed.

The robot led them to a staircase they had missed earlier, having not explored this area far. It went down. They followed, Zareen finding herself immediately next to Didier, with Ghada and Emad practically growling at Bertrand.

The assassin had a limp he'd concealed earlier, but one that made Zareen feel better. It might keep him from misbehaving.

At least until they were outside.

What did Finn expect to happen at that point?

Quickly, they made their way to the discontinuity in the architecture representing those spaces that the Durren had added later, hiding away from the Control System or unable to awaken it.

Something. Hopefully Asher had found out more details that, like Finn, he didn't wish to share with Didier and the others.

Still, their guide led Finn, who never once looked back to see if everyone was with him.

But the Spartans were there when she looked, holding the

rear, so she supposed that nobody would be allowed to turn back like Lot's wife.

Ahead, she saw sunlight. The entrance that Asher had been able to open when Ghada had found the hidden door.

Shambala, though not even remotely what she had been expecting.

What had she thought to find?

Zareen supposed that she'd find a Durren base, filled with people she could talk to. Convince to assist her somehow.

Not that she would be immediately hauled to the border and ordered to depart.

And Finn seemingly had a plan, so she simply had to trust the man.

Trust her moral compass.

Of course.

That brought an even greater smile to her face.

Daylight.

Late afternoon, with shadows stretching.

The robot guide stepped onto the platform and turned to face them, like a shepherd counting his flock as the ten of them emerged.

"Thank you, Finn," it said, then immediately returned to the entrance and walked away.

Zareen found herself behind a wall of bodies, with Didier and his compatriots far too close, but still separated.

"Here's the deal," Finn told everyone. "Machine in there is going to destroy itself to keep its secrets from falling into human hands. Like Asher originally, it is programmed not to hurt people, so it had to get us gone before it did anything, but it wants us to leave. We're going to. Beauchêne, I can't speak for you, but everyone here is unarmed at the moment. I propose that we all hike down to the aircraft, board, and leave. You want to come back later, that's on your head, but that is exactly what we're going to do. And there's enough sun that we can get there and take off in daylight. Questions?"

"You are simply abandoning all this?" the blonde woman demanded shrewishly.

Fraulein Reiher. Didier utterly loathed the woman from the way he looked at her. Zareen didn't have a much better opinion.

"That's right," Finn nodded. "That was the deal. We got to safety, then we were on our own. If we tried to go back, then he couldn't promise we wouldn't be hurt. I intent to live to fight another day. Zareen?"

She studied his face. She wasn't sure what she saw, but it was clear that he wanted to leave. Insisted. When normally he and the others willingly accepted her decisions.

But she had told the Control System that he was her moral compass.

Had she gone astray?

Perhaps, given how close she had gotten to her dream. Maybe she needed to listen to the man.

"Yes, Finn," she agreed. "What about our camp?"

"There anything you'll miss if we abandon it?" he asked.

Zareen did a quick mental survey.

"A few things in the chest, that's all," she replied.

"I can carry the chest," Asher volunteered. "And I agree that most of the rest can be left, as it represents things we picked up in Lahore for this trip."

Didier and his trio stood in the doorway. Zareen could see a few metal backs, already distant and receding with every step.

"Didier?" Finn asked.

"You people are fools," the Frenchman scorned them. "If the machine in charge cannot hurt us, why do we not return and take anything we can lay our hands on?"

"That's on you, Didier," Finn replied evenly. "See you later."

And he started walking down the stairs. Not quite at the killing pace he'd marched earlier, but not pausing for any reason.

Nor once looking back.

A man on a mission.

What mission?

Zareen caught up with him as they descended from the mountain.

"What's going on?" she asked quietly, eyes focused on the steps so she didn't slip and break her neck at this late stage.

"Machine in there is going to blow up the whole mountain to keep humans from finding anything out about the Durren or the Etulfvik," Finn grinned.

"And you just let Didier and the others walk back into that?" she demanded hotly.

His grin never wavered.

"I got them to safety, like the robot asked me to, Zareen," he said. "Outside. Nobody was armed, so we couldn't start shooting at each other, 'cause fists don't count. At that point, I made the decision that we're too close and needed to return to the plane and fly away to safety. Didier and his chumps decided to return to the facility, where I suspect they'll get caught up in whatever happens, and maybe get themselves killed. It was that, or a Mexican Standoff when we got to the planes, with no idea who they'd left down in the basin."

"So you killed them for me?" she asked, aghast at his behavior.

Even when provoked, he had only shot Bertrand to wound, rather than through the heart.

"Nope," he said. "They're killing themselves because they weren't smart enough to listen. Too greedy, which at the end of the day is most of the reason the Durren and others don't trust us."

"You are a wicked man, Finn," Emad offered. "That is a most lovely trap you have caused them to fall into. Will they be killed?"

"Machine in charge didn't feel like the kind of fellow that was gonna do things halfway, ya know?"

Zareen did know. She'd gotten that impression from the machine while speaking with it.

Cruel and unyielding.

How had Finn gotten through to it? And what did it mean that they had talked about the nature of evil, the two of them?

She found herself looking forward to his explanation, once they got to safety.

CHAPTER FORTY-SEVEN

Finn studied the view.

Two aircraft.

From here, it almost looked like *Sunrise* parked next to the old California Condor, but he knew better. There'd be a big, nasty swastika on the tail, announcing the travelers to anyone who cared to look. Almost made him wish he had a gun right now, but it would come down to him and the others running one hell of a bluff.

At least they could get reasonably close as the sunlight got long. One tent between the aircraft, where wings and bodies might keep some wind and rain off. Nobody on watch at the moment outside, but there might be one in a cold, metal aircraft.

Finn looked around. Asher had the trunk like a duffel bag over one shoulder. Ghada had her knives. Rest of them had their sneakiness.

He focused on Emad.

"Need you to do to them what you did to me, that first time," Finn told the guy.

Emad grinned.

"With pleasure," he said. "How many should we expect?"

Finn turned to Hans.

"Radio operator?" he asked.

"Probably kept him and left off the navigator/bombardier," Hans answered. "Still, I'd guess two, but be prepared for a third. Too cold to sleep in the plane up here, so in that tent."

"Excellent," Emad said. "Ghada, if you would care to accompany me?"

She laughed quietly and Finn watched those two start their stalk.

He gave them a lead, then nodded to the others to follow him.

They'd slipped sideways coming out of that canyon mouth, in case someone was watching their original trail, and were coming in from closer to twelve o'clock.

With surprise, he hoped, because Finn hadn't seen any radios with Didier's folks.

Nobody visible as they got close, which just meant nobody on watch. Made things easier.

Emad and Ghada got close to the tent, while Finn circled towards the Heinkel, which was closer. Worse come to worst, he could stop someone from boarding the HE-111 and getting to the machine guns.

Emad stopped, then slipped sideways and Finn saw him with a rifle in his hands, like maybe they'd stacked them outside of the tent instead of in with them. Dumb, considering how cold it might get up here, but not his problem.

Ghada had a rifle as well, so Finn felt better.

Then Emad fired a shot into the air, the two of them stepping back and aiming at the tent.

"Come out with your hands up or we will shoot you dead," the man yelled in a voice accustomed to being listened to.

Finn grinned.

Two men stumbled out a few moments later. From the looks of them, maybe they'd been into the schnapps a bit this afternoon.

"Any more?" he demanded in German.

"*Nein!*"

"Step over there," Emad gestured.

Finn watched Ghada peek into the tent and nod, so he started walking that way.

The two air crew were recruiting-poster slick. Tall, lean, blond. Dressed in gray with flight suits.

"*Was is los?*" the nearer one demanded, so Finn switched to German to talk to them.

"Your friends have decided to remain inside the mountain," Finn said. "We wanted to go home, so we came down here. You can wait for them for a bit or…"

He lost all words when the afternoon behind him lit up with a dull red glow. Everybody fell silent, watching the way the cloud of smoke rose like a big mushroom growing over there.

Sound and wind arrived not long after that. Not enough of either to matter, once it got here.

"Okay, so I was wrong," Finn finally said when everything quieted down again. "Dunno what they did, but it just might be that they aren't coming back after all. Because I didn't want any misunderstandings, we're going to go aboard our plane, get it ready, then take off and leave, while you two gentleman stand right here. If you don't give me any reason, you won't get hurt, then tomorrow you can see if your friends got out of that alive. If they did, you're here for them. If not, you should carry news back to wherever you came from. Understand me?"

They both nodded in shock. Not a lot you can do when someone has the drop on you like that.

"Hans," he said simply.

"*Ja,*" the big kraut said, then walked over to *Sunrise* to start fixing the things he'd done so nobody could steal it while they were gone.

Finn considered disabling the Heinkel, but he didn't figure that was nice.

Might even be evil, at the end of the day.

Can't have that.

Wasn't like Beauchêne and his friends were likely to be a problem in the future, and these two hadn't done anything to Finn.

"Zareen, you and Asher get aboard and ready to go," Finn ordered next.

"You two will sit down and remain seated," Emad said to the pilots. "If you do, you won't be hurt."

Finn nodded. Emad and Ghada had that covered.

Time to get the plane running and haul ass out of here. If Didier and the others had changed their mind, they might be coming. Good thing Emad and Ghada were the only ones armed at the moment, assuming Zareen didn't settle in the 20mm Type 99 cannon in the rear dorsal turret to have an opinion.

He got into the cockpit after a rigorous preflight. Never know what strangers might have done, and they were in the middle of nowhere up here.

All good.

"Finn, start it up," Hans yelled, so Finn got the engines going.

Cold, but not too bad. Warmed up pretty quick.

Ghada was watching, so he motioned her to board. She and Emad kept the rifles and crab walked, but the two Germans didn't look like a threat.

Everyone aboard and closed up, Finn opened the throttles and lined up with the setting sun.

As he got off the ground, *Sunrise* ran like a mustang, climbing hard and fast.

If he ignored the compass, it was just like flying into the sunrise, too.

That felt right.

CHAPTER FORTY-EIGHT

Zareen had moved forward and swapped places with Hans, once the two men got the aircraft aloft. They were not, however, headed southwest, which they should have been, had they been returning to Lahore, so she presumed Finn had been lying to Didier and the others, just in case. A little north of west.

She approved.

Headphones on so she could talk over the engine noise, she studied the man.

"What did you and the Control System discuss, Finn?" Zareen asked. "You described it as the nature of evil."

"You'd told it that I was your moral compass," Finn glanced over. "We talked about that. I had to quote a little Epicurus at it, then I might have called it evil and demanded that it do something about it."

Zareen gasped. Finn had *demanded*?

But it was Finn. He was like that. Brutally deliberate when he needed to be, and certain of himself in ways that most folks were not.

Including herself, when she would perhaps veer too close to evil outcomes.

"And that required he blow up the mountain?" she pressed.

"Humans are generally too dangerous to know about the Durren or Etulfvik," Finn said, hands still smooth and sure on the controls as she watched. "Fellow couldn't kill us, but didn't want us stripping the place like the Durren had done, so he was all set to shove us out the front door before he did his deed. I suppose that he could have closed up that hatch when we were all outside. Or told the robots to stop Didier from going back in, but it all comes down to free will at that point, and I got the impression that he didn't like the Frenchie all that much, either."

"I presume that he was monitoring all conversations," Zareen nodded. "Thus, he would have heard us discuss empires. That probably didn't help Didier's cause. But he still killed the others."

"I'm guessing he had a fuse and he lit it, Zareen," Finn said, turning so deadly serious that she gasped again. "Nothing much he could do to stop it at that point, and he and I had made sure that everyone was safe in that moment. Didier and the Nazis chose to go back in, knowing that they weren't welcome, so maybe they'd turned into rats and cockroaches at that point. Dunno. Do know that we've confirmed at least one Etulfvik base that the Durren had known about, so I gotta guess there might be others out there, waiting for someone to find them."

The way he stared at her spoke volumes. He would be there as she searched. As would the others.

Even Emad, meaning that they would need to have *that* conversation.

Zareen found herself looking forward to it.

A thought struck her that caused her smile to grow so big that even a big, tough man like Finn Severijns flinched a little.

"What?" he demanded quietly.

"How many stops would you need to make, in order to get us to Glasgow, Finn?" she asked.

His recoil was a thing of utter joy to her, but she supposed that all of them had heard her stories about her dread and dangerous grandmother, Olivia MacQuaid, though she still thought that her father would have louder opinions, at least on Emad al-Sadri.

Not that she would listen. In fact, Zareen wondered if the biggest problem might be keeping Grandmother Olivia from demanding to join them on the next leg of this quest.

She could be like that.

"Maybe four thousand miles from here," he said finally. "Depending on wind and weather, probably three stops, just to be safe. Want to get us down off the plateau first. Then to Kabul, where we can reset the engines for a lower altitude. Beirut would be my preference along the Med from there. Short enough flight, and that puts Rome and Paris both in easy distance of Sunrise's big tanks as long as we don't stay long enough for an ex-wife to find me. Stop there and get a little cleaned up before we go meet Grandma, if that's okay?"

"More than okay, Finn," she smiled. "I'll need to cable her that we're coming anyway, so that she has time to prepare. And from Beirut, I can contact a few other folks and update them."

Zareen pulled off the headphones and hung them on their hook, then stood up and kissed Finn on the top of his head before heading aft.

Tibet had been something of a bust, at the end of the day, other than it had greatly expanded her knowledge of what was possible. And hopefully Asher would have more details that he could share, from his dense conversations with the Control System.

Then, anything might be possible. Tunguska was probably pointless at this juncture. Similarly, the Curuçá River event in Brazil in 1930.

But she knew that the Etulfvik had been here for a while. And the Durren had made maps, presumably encoded such that only other Durren could read them.

Or explorers who spoke the language.

Zareen smiled at her friends as she settled aft and considered what languages she might learn next. China had been a relatively stable civilization for thousands of years at this point, which was presumably why there was a base in Tibet. Close to both there and the Fertile Crescent.

So much she could do. So much she could learn.

But first, yes, Olivia would have opinions. Nigel as well, but Father was retired, presumably.

It was up to Zareen to discover the truth.

Whatever was out there.

CHAPTER FORTY-NINE

Didier awoke with a start, unable to reconcile where he was.

Hell, already?

Likely his final destination.

He groaned with aches and pains. Someone turned a lamp up. Light revealed a hut of some sort. Leather walls and ceiling. Furs around him and under him.

Bertrand appeared in front of him. Over him, as Didier was flat on his back.

Bertrand looked like he had been mugged. Black eye reaching clear down to his jaw. Hair shaved off on one side with a wound covered in cloth wrapped around his skull.

Bertrand's smile was pained, even.

"Where am I?" Didier croaked.

"Villagers found us," Bertrand said. "When the mountain exploded, I managed to dig you out, but the Germans had gone ahead and vanished. Dragged you as far as the camp Shirazi had left. Folks came along after that, talking about two aircraft leaving, so the German pilots thought we were dead. I thought we were dead."

"Are you sure we aren't?" Didier asked.

Every breath hurt. Every eye blink.

Bertrand nodded. He looked like that hurt.

"I don't speak Tibetan, or whatever it is," he replied. "They've treated us both, and fed us. It's been about four days, I think. You caught a fever and a tiny, ancient woman treated you. I'm supposed to get her when you wake up. Do we know what we're doing next?"

Didier nodded.

The woman and her gangster friend had tricked them, but Didier was willing to own that. His own greed and stupidity had overwhelmed him, and he could have flown away when they did.

Safely.

At least the *Fraulein* and her pet Konrad were presumably dead and in whichever of the hells best suited them.

Good riddance.

"We will heal," Didier told his assassin. "Then we will figure out how we can escape Tibet. Afghanistan is not far away. Nor is British India. I have no interest in Russian lands, but we might be able to get to Khotan in China, then find our way either east or west, depending. For now, we recover, then, we will get home."

Bertrand nodded again and slipped outside the tent. Hut. Whatever it was.

Didier would need time. Precious time where Shirazi and her companions might steal another march on him, but at least next time he wouldn't have to share anything with the Germans.

Or anybody.

READ MORE!

Be sure to read all the books in the Air Pirates of Cyrenaica series!
https://www.knottedroadpress.com/product-category/science-fiction/air-pirates-of-cyrenaica/

ABOUT THE AUTHOR

Blaze Ward writes science fiction in the Alexandria Station universe (Jessica Keller, The Science Officer, Phil Kosnett, etc.) as well as several other science fiction universes, such as Corsac Fox, Operation Marrakesh, and more. He also writes odd bits of high fantasy with swords and orcs. In addition, he is the Editor and Publisher of *Boundary Shock Quarterly Magazine*. You can find out more at his website www.blazeward.com, as well as Facebook, Goodreads, and other places.

Blaze's works are available as ebooks, paper, and audio, and can be found at a variety of online vendors. His newsletter comes out regularly, and you can also follow his blog on his website. He really enjoys interacting with fans, and looks forward to any and all questions—even ones about his books!

Never miss a release!
If you'd like to be notified of new releases, sign up for my newsletter.

http://www.blazeward.com/newsletter/

Buy More!
Did you know that you can buy directly from the KRP website?

https://www.knottedroadpress.com/shop/

Connect with Blaze!

Web: www.blazeward.com
Boundary Shock Quarterly (BSQ):
https://www.boundaryshockquarterly.com/

ABOUT KNOTTED ROAD PRESS

Knotted Road Press publishes dynamic fiction set in exotic locations and unique non-fiction voices in genres such as autobiography, business, cookbooks, and how-to. Our authors cover a wide range of genres including science fiction, fantasy, mystery, literary, and poetry, appealing to all readers. We offer both DRM-free ebooks and print books for a global readership.

Knotted Road Press
www.KnottedRoadPress.com
www.KnottedRoadPress.com/Shop

www.ingramcontent.com/pod-product-compliance
Lightning Source LLC
Chambersburg PA
CBHW070534100726
47907CB00004B/1116